"Does you

He must know,
sneaking around on the guy. She wasn't like that.

She gave him a quick, startled glance. "How did you know I'd remarried?"

"It wasn't exactly a secret on base. There were plenty of people who didn't mind passing along the information. It took a while to get to Afghanistan, but I heard it."

She nodded. "You didn't hear all of it. David died more than three years ago. A hit and run."

Nate hadn't let himself think of her married to another man, but he didn't like the fact that she was on her own again, either. "You're right. I didn't hear that. I'm sorry."

"Thank you," she said with quiet dignity.

"Who told you I was back in Riley's Cove? You haven't been in touch with anyone in my family. They'd have told me."

"I checked with your old unit. Sergeant Harris is still there. He said you'd moved back to Michigan…I'm sorry," she said, looking down at the lake. "I know you'd planned to make the Army your career."

"It was time for me to go." He'd made it safely through three tours, but his luck had run out two days before his unit shipped home from Iraq. A nineteen-year-old Earnhardt wannabe in a Humvee, anxious as hell to be on the plane back to the States, had pinned him against a loading dock, breaking his knee and crushing his ankle. He'd been damn lucky not to lose half his leg. "You didn't come all this way from Texas just to offer your sympathy for something that happened eighteen months ago. Why are you here, Sarah?"

"I need you to marry me."

Dear Reader,

Nate and Sarah loved each other deeply, but their inability to agree on having a child destroyed their marriage. Now, four years later, Sarah has come to Cottonwood Lake, Michigan, to ask Nate to marry her again, and raise her fatherless three-year-old son. Nate agrees because Sarah is dying.

But what happens when she doesn't die, and they find themselves bound to each other once more, a family in name only?

Marriage by Necessity is a story of two people working their way through a tangle of old hurts to forge a future together.

We hope you enjoy your trip to Cottonwood Lake. It's one of those places we love to write about, filled with good times, good food, good fun and good people.

Enjoy,

Carol and *Marion (Marisa Carroll)*

MARRIAGE BY NECESSITY
Marisa Carroll

HARLEQUIN®

TORONTO • NEW YORK • LONDON
AMSTERDAM • PARIS • SYDNEY • HAMBURG
STOCKHOLM • ATHENS • TOKYO • MILAN • MADRID
PRAGUE • WARSAW • BUDAPEST • AUCKLAND

ISBN 0-373-71306-1

MARRIAGE BY NECESSITY

Copyright © 2005 by Carol I. Wagner and Marian L. Franz.

All rights reserved. Except for use in any review, the reproduction or utilization of this work in whole or in part in any form by any electronic, mechanical or other means, now known or hereafter invented, including xerography, photocopying and recording, or in any information storage or retrieval system, is forbidden without the written permission of the publisher, Harlequin Enterprises Limited, 225 Duncan Mill Road, Don Mills, Ontario, Canada M3B 3K9.

All characters in this book have no existence outside the imagination of the author and have no relation whatsoever to anyone bearing the same name or names. They are not even distantly inspired by any individual known or unknown to the author, and all incidents are pure invention.

This edition published by arrangement with Harlequin Books S.A.

® and TM are trademarks of the publisher. Trademarks indicated with ® are registered in the United States Patent and Trademark Office, the Canadian Trade Marks Office and in other countries.

www.eHarlequin.com

Printed in U.S.A.

Marriage by Necessity

CHAPTER ONE

COTTONWOOD LAKE was quiet today, its blue-gray surface as smooth as glass. Sarah closed her eyes and heard the sound of a boat starting up far out on the lake, and closer, the scolding chatter of a squirrel in the tree beside her car. The autumn sun was warm on her face and shoulders as it filtered through the branches of yellow-leaved cottonwoods. It was a perfect southern Michigan Indian summer afternoon.

Far too lovely a day to think about dying.

But she had no choice. She must talk to Nate today. She couldn't come this far only to turn around and go back to their dreary little motel room in Ann Arbor. She had to drive up the sandy, unpaved lane, past the fork in the road that led to Riley's Trailer Trash Campground, to the top of the hill, and ask her ex-husband to marry her again.

She tightened her fingers around the steering wheel of the secondhand minivan. She hadn't seen or talked to Nate in almost four years, not since he'd shipped off to Afghanistan in the wake of the September 11th attacks. Their marriage was already on life support by then and war and distance had done nothing to heal the wound. The divorce had become final while he was still overseas. Nate had wanted it that way. So had she, at least she thought she had.

She no longer had the luxury of what-ifs.

She had a child to protect and provide for.

Another man's child. Her late husband, David Taylor's son.

She half turned in her seat to stare at the sleeping toddler who was the center of her world. The movement sent a wave of prickly sensation down the right side of her body, followed by a sudden numbness. She sucked in her breath and rubbed her fingers over her worn jeans. She couldn't feel the fabric or the skin beneath. She turned her hand over and looked at the palm where the skin was reddened from this morning's dumb accident. She hadn't even felt the scalding water. No pain, no heat, no cold. The loss of sensation was only one of the symptoms of the deadly growth that was rapidly twining itself around her spinal cord, already threatening to burrow into her brain. The risky and complicated surgery to remove it was scheduled in a week's time. She would need that long to complete the legal arrangements for a wedding.

If Nate agreed to her plan.

He had to. She had no one else to raise her son if—

She cut off the panicky thought. Not now. Save that terrifying scenario for the wakeful hours of the night when she was too tired to keep the fear at bay.

Now she had to be strong. For Matthew's sake. For his future.

NATE FOWLER grabbed a rag and wiped the grease from his fingers. "Just a minute. I'm coming!" he hollered over his shoulder. He'd never had people banging on his door asking to see his bikes before his sixteen-year-old cousin, Erika, designed a Web site for him as a school project. Turning away from the 1938 Indian Four motorcycle he was rebuilding for a wealthy collector in Detroit, he limped across the scarred, wide-planked wooden floor of the hundred-year-old barn that was his workshop, and he hoped someday, his home. He flung open the small side door. "What can I do for—Sarah?"

"Hello, Nate."

His ex-wife was the last person on earth he expected to see standing there. He stared at her for a moment. She was just as pretty as he remembered. Her hair was shorter now, no longer the riot of cinnamon-brown curls it had been when they were married, but still shiny and fine as silk, just brushing the curve of her chin and the collar of her apple-green sweater. Her figure was more mature, too, her breasts a little heavier, her hips more rounded, but like the hairstyle, it suited her.

"I…I hope I'm not interrupting your work," she said as his silence dragged out.

"What are you doing here, Sarah?" His voice sounded as gruff as his granddad's, but there was nothing he could do about it, even if he'd wanted to. The shock of seeing her again after all this time overrode everything. She looked at him with the same big brown eyes that had attracted him to her that spring day eight years earlier, as she waited tables at the little restaurant outside Fort Hood, where he'd been stationed. He'd just earned his sergeant's stripes and had gone there for coffee and eggs after an all-night celebration with a couple of the other newly minted NCOs. It was a spur-of-the-moment decision that had changed his life.

"I need to talk to you." Nate glanced down at her left hand. She wasn't wearing a wedding ring. But she had remarried. He'd heard that much after their divorce. As a matter of fact if the gossip on the base was right, she'd barely waited for the ink to dry on their divorce papers before she'd tied the knot.

"We don't have anything to talk about."

She winced at the coldness in his voice but held her ground. "I know you aren't happy to see me, but please, hear me out." He caught the sheen of tears in her eyes and tensed. She'd always cried easily, but she didn't let them fall now. And there was a veneer of steel overlying her soft words he'd never heard before. "It's important, Nate. Please."

He hesitated. Indecision like that would've gotten him killed in the old days. You didn't last long in Explosive Ordnance Disposal if you couldn't keep your mind on your business. He began to process information one thread at a time. Did she want money? She hadn't wanted any four years ago. Money was one thing they'd never fought about during their short marriage. The wedge that had split them apart had been far more serious. He would've given her every cent he had. What he wouldn't give her was a child. He still thought he'd done the right thing then, refusing to go off to war leaving her pregnant and alone in the world. But she'd been too young and insecure to realize it, and he'd done one hell of a lousy job trying to explain his reasons. The nagging awareness of his past failings softened his next words. "Come on in. We can talk inside."

Sarah glanced over her shoulder at the seen-better-days minivan parked beneath the big oak at the edge of the drive. "I'd rather stay out here if you don't mind." She made a little gesture toward the two folding lawn chairs propped against the side of the barn where his granddad, Harmon Riley, liked to sit and watch the sunset with a cigar in one hand and a beer in the other.

"All right." He took a couple of limping steps and unfolded one of the chairs for her, setting it next to the sun-warmed foundation stones. He waited until she was seated then stuffed the shop rag into the back pocket of his paint-stained jeans and lowered himself onto the sagging webbing of the second chair. She folded her hands in her lap, staring at her vehicle.

"Does your husband know you're here?" he asked. He must know, Nate surmised. He couldn't see Sarah sneaking around on the guy. She wasn't like that.

She gave him a quick, startled glance. "How did you know I'd remarried?"

"It wasn't exactly a secret on base. There were plenty of people who didn't mind passing along the information. It took awhile to get to Afghanistan, but I heard it."

She nodded. "You didn't hear all of it. David died more than three years ago. A hit-and-run driver in the parking lot of the store he managed."

He hadn't let himself think of her married to another man, but he didn't like that she was on her own again, either. "You're right, I didn't hear that. I'm sorry."

"Thank you," she said with quiet dignity.

"Who told you I was back in Riley's Cove? You haven't been in touch with anyone in the family. They would have told me if you had."

"I checked with your old unit. Sergeant Harris is still there. He told me you'd left the Army and moved back to Michigan."

Ennis Harris had been his best friend for twelve years. They'd been buddies since basic training, serving together in Kosovo, Afghanistan and Iraq. But since his accident and subsequent early retirement they'd lost touch. His fault, not Ennis's.

"I didn't know what happened until just recently," she said, looking down the hill to the view of the lake. "I'm sorry. I know you'd planned to make the Army your career."

"It was time for me to go." He'd made it safely through three tours in war zones but his luck had run out two days before his unit shipped home from Iraq. A nineteen-year-old Earnhardt wanna-be in a Humvee, anxious as hell to be on the plane back to the States, had pinned him against a loading dock breaking his knee and crushing his ankle. He'd been damned lucky not to lose half his leg. He didn't want to talk about his accident or the aftermath. "You didn't come all the way from Texas just to offer your sympathy for something that happened eighteen months ago. Why are you here, Sarah?"

"I need you to marry me."

SARAH WISHED she could take back the bald statement the moment it left her lips. She was going about it all wrong. She'd planned this so carefully, laid out her argument logically and methodically, but when it came time to put her resolve to the test she'd acted impulsively, speaking from her heart, as she had so often during their marriage. Nate was frowning. The double furrow between his brows was more pronounced than it had been four years ago. Otherwise he looked much the same, thick dark hair, gray eyes, broad shoulders. Solid, earthy, sure of himself and his place in the world.

"Marry you? Is this some kind of joke?"

Sarah took a deep breath and tried to slow her racing heart. She didn't have much time. Matty would be waking up any moment. He always fell asleep in the car, lulled by the engine and the passing scenery. But he never slept for long after the car stopped. She needed to plead her case to Nate without the distraction of an active three-year-old.

"I know it seems crazy, an impossible favor, but believe me, Nate, if I had anyone else to turn to I would. I'm desperate." She licked her lips. It was never easy to say the words so she rushed to get them out without stumbling. "I...I might be dying. And I have no one to care for my son."

He went very still, his face as shell-shocked as her own must've looked when she first heard the prognosis. Then his expression cleared and, his voice level and controlled, he said, "Let's take this one step at a time. You have a child?"

She glanced toward the car. "Yes. A little boy. Matthew. He's three." She could leave Matty in the van for a few more minutes. She'd been careful to park in the shade so the car would stay cool. He was safely fastened into his car seat. He'd be okay.

Nate's veneer of disinterested calm cracked for a moment. "You must have gotten pregnant right after our divorce."

She gave him back look for look. "I got pregnant right after I remarried."

"I didn't mean it as an insult." Nate apologized automatically, once more in control of his emotions.

Still, she'd remarried only a week after their divorce. She'd gone to work at the HomeContractor store in Killeen, where David Taylor was the assistant manager, right after Nate left for Afghanistan. She'd been lonely and alone and her marriage was over. So when David fell in love with her, she'd tried to love him back, she'd tried so very hard.

"David was a good man, Nate. He would've been a loving husband and father to our son, but he never had the chance."

Nate stood abruptly and the unexpectedness of his movement drew Sarah awkwardly from her chair as well. He shoved his hands in his pockets and stared down at the ground for a long moment, gathering his thoughts. It was a habit of his, she remembered, and it had always irritated her when she was bubbling over with words. But she'd learned something about patience over the last three, hard years and waited for him to speak. "What's wrong with you, Sarah?" he said at last. "Do you have cancer?"

"I have a growth, here on my spine." She touched the back of her neck. "It's not malignant. Not the way cancer is. What it's called doesn't matter. The name's so long I can't even pronounce it. The doctors in Texas didn't even want to attempt the surgery. They referred me up here to a Doctor Jamison at the university. Have you heard of her?"

Nate shook his head

"It doesn't matter. The odds are less than fifty percent she'll be able to remove the entire growth. I might wake up paralyzed. I…I might not wake up at all."

His hands came out of his pockets. For a moment she thought he might take her in his arms. She took a step back. She'd always remembered how wonderful it felt to be held by him, although while she was married to David, she'd buried the memory so deeply she almost believed she'd forgotten. She'd break down and give in to the terrible fear inside her if he showed her any tenderness at all. "I'm not asking you to be responsible for me if I'm not able to take care of myself. I…I've made arrangements." She would tell him later, all the details of insurance and long-term care facilities, of living wills and "do not resuscitate" orders. She didn't dare dwell on herself, on what might lie in store for her. It was Matty she had to safeguard.

He gripped the back of the lawn chair and leaned slightly forward. "Good God, Sarah, listen to yourself. Do you know what you're asking? We ended up divorced because we couldn't agree on having children. Why in God's name would you trust me with your son?" His jaw tightened. He looked fierce and rock hard. And sad. Beneath the surface anger his eyes were dark with sorrow and loss, she would swear it.

"You're a kind man. You'll make a fantastic father." She couldn't stop a small, bittersweet smile. "I always knew that about you even if you didn't know it yourself." She kept on talking, not giving him a chance to deny it. "I know I could ask you to just be his guardian but that takes time, filings, court hearings, all those things. Until all of that was settled he would have to be placed in foster care." She faltered a little over those words but kept going. "The lawyer said…it would be simpler if we were married. That it would be easier for you to make decisions for Matty if I'm not able to care for him." This time she couldn't stop the quaver in her voice. She didn't know which nightmare was more terrifying. Death, quick and painless as it would be, or the alternative, the possibility of paralysis or years and years in a vegetative state, dependent on others for everything, while Matty grew up alone and unwanted, the way she had.

"He needs you, Nate. There's no one else. David's only sister is a single mother. Her youngest has Down syndrome. Matthew's grandfather is in the early stages of Alzheimer's. Carrie, my sister-in-law, has him to care for, too. And I…" She let the sentence trail off. Nate knew she was an orphan, abandoned at birth. She'd bounced around from one foster home to another throughout her childhood. She didn't need to remind him of the loneliness and heartache of her youth. "The only family I ever really had was you."

CHAPTER TWO

"I WONDERED HOW LONG it was going to take you to get yourself down the hill and tell me what's going on at your place. Where you been all day?" Harmon Riley, bundled up in an ancient buffalo plaid wool coat and with a vintage Tigers cap covering his nearly bald head, was seated in an old metal lawn chair in front of the fire he built on the lakeshore most nights it wasn't raining or blowing too hard. A plastic cooler sat on the ground beside him. His old tom, Buster, was curled up on his lap. The cat opened one eye, stared at Nate suspiciously for a moment, and then went back to sleep.

"I had business in Ann Arbor."

"Don't you mean *we* had business in Ann Arbor? I didn't see that minivan with the out-of-state plates take off and leave, did I?"

"No. It's still here."

"So's the woman that was driving it yesterday, eh? Not like you to have overnight guests. At least not the kind you don't bring down to introduce to your old granddad. Sit down. You give me a crick in my neck standing there like that."

Nate did as he was told and Harm handed him a beer from the cooler. He twisted off the top and took a swallow, then cradled the longneck with one hand and stared past the fire at the lights of the yacht club on the other side of the lake.

"This overnight guest anyone I know?" the old man asked bluntly, making no attempt to hide his curiosity. Subtlety was not a Riley family trait. Just ask any of the members of the Cottonwood Lake Development Committee. They wanted to gentrify the hamlet of Riley's Cove just like the lawyers and doctors and the professors from the university were doing to Lakeview, the larger town that sprawled along the north shore of the lake. But the stubborn old man, who'd lived in Riley's Cove all his life, wanted nothing to do with upscale condos and art galleries, and even, God help them, a Starbucks.

Harm wanted things to stay the way they were. Simple and fairly inexpensive and quiet eight months out of twelve. So there was no way he would give in to the committee and move the dozen or so campers and travel trailers he rented back from the lakefront, or tear down the rickety boathouse at the edge of the property. And most defiantly of all, he would not hear of upgrading the name of his establishment. Riley's Trailer Trash Campground was here to stay.

"It's Sarah, Granddad."

"I'll be darned. Sarah? I thought she looked familiar but I don't see as good as I used to, so I couldn't be sure. Never figured to see her here again, though." He shook his head. "Sarah. She's got a little one with her, I noticed. Boy or girl?"

"A little boy. His name is Matthew and he's three."

"Hard to tell these days the way they dress them alike. Does he favor her?" Harmon picked up his cigar from the cut-down coffee can that served as an ashtray and took a long pull. Nate watched its ember glow red and then fade. Disturbed by the movement, or maybe just because he didn't like the smell of tobacco smoke, the old cat jumped stiffly down off Harm's lap and stalked away into the shadows along the shoreline, tail held high.

"He looks a lot like her except he's blond and his eyes are blue, not brown. He's a sturdy little kid, but not real big for his age."

"Three, you say? Same age as Tessa's hellion. Don't know how your sister copes with that one! Sarah's not here to tell you he's yours, is she?" The old man's voice had gentled but Nate pretended not to notice.

"You know he's not mine." The words were hard to get out. He would like to have a son. He'd never thought too much about having children before the blowup with Sarah. And afterward? There didn't seem much point especially considering what he'd learned about himself after the accident. "She married again right after the divorce. Her husband's dead, killed by a hit-and-run driver in a goddamned store parking lot before the baby was born."

"That's a darned shame, but why'd she show up here after all this time? Don't make sense to my way of thinking. Want to tell me about it? Might help later on. Your mother's going to ask much tougher questions than I am." Harmon rolled the cigar between his gnarled fingers, then looked over at Nate. "She's been up here twice today trying to nose out what's going on. She's not going to be thrilled to hear it's Sarah come calling."

"I'll talk to Mom and Dad first thing tomorrow. There've been a lot of details to work out today."

"Details? What kind of details?"

Nate leaned his head back and looked up at the night sky. He couldn't see many stars, he'd been staring at the fire too long, but the harvest moon hung low over the lake, yellow and immense. He loved this time of year, the colors, the smells, the slow retreat of summer's warmth that almost hid the quiet, stealthy approach of winter. He took a few moments to order his thoughts. His grandfather stubbed the butt of his cigar into the sand in the coffee can and waited patiently. The cigar smoke drifted away and was replaced by the tang of a wood fire.

"Sarah's ill," he said at last. "Some kind of growth on her spinal cord the doctors aren't sure they'll be able to remove. When she learned the best doctor was here in Ann Arbor at the university, she got the idea of us getting married again so I could take care of Matthew if…the worst happens." He might have been giving his CO a status report back in the old days. It was easier that way, not thinking about everything that could go wrong. *To imagine Sarah dead, or paralyzed, unable to care for herself. A fate he was certain held more fear for her than death.*

"Hell's bells," Harm said. For all his rough edges he'd never been one to cuss up a storm. "I didn't figure that. That's a darned shame. It ain't fair having to face dying so young, just like your Grandma, God rest her soul. Are you going to do it? Just like that, up and take responsibility for her boy?"

"She's alone in the world, Granddad. How can I say no?"

"A lot of men would. Bringing up a kid on your own. That's about the hardest thing you can do." Harm had raised Nate's mother and her younger brother by himself after his wife died of kidney failure. He'd done a good job with both of them, but Nate knew it couldn't have been easy. Especially back in the days when single fathers were few and far between.

"You did it. And not one kid, but two. Mom and Uncle Dan turned out just fine."

"They were mine," Harm said bluntly. "Not some other man's child. That might make a powerful difference down the line."

"I can't let that stop me. She's got no one, Granddad. I loved her once. If I can do this for her now, I will. She wants a family for the boy, and a father. I don't know if I'll be any good at the job, but I've got to try. We applied for the marriage license this afternoon. The wedding's Friday. Her surgery is Saturday morning at University Hospital."

"So soon? Don't give you much time to make up your mind. Only, it sounds like you already have."

"The way I see things, it was the only choice I had."

He and Sarah had talked for a long time the night before after Matty fell asleep on the couch. Or, more accurately, he had let her talk, outlining in minute detail all the arrangements she'd made for Matthew's future. She wouldn't be a financial burden, she insisted. And neither would her son.

That was when she'd asked him if there was a woman in his life. He had thought briefly of green eyes, a smattering of freckles, the brush of tapered fingers over the surface of an antique rocking horse, then dismissed the image. "There's no one," he had said, and meant it. Sarah had ducked her head for a moment. He suspected she had done that to hide the relief that hadn't quite faded from her eyes when she looked up again.

"I…I should have thought to ask you that earlier," she said.

"I would have told you earlier if it had been a problem."

She had nodded and stood up, swaying just a little. "It's getting late. We should go."

"Why don't you stay here tonight," he'd offered before he could change his mind. "It's too late for you to be driving back to Ann Arbor. You're not used to country roads and there will be fog in the low spots." She was pale, he noticed, and there were dark shadows under her eyes. Sarah had never been sick when they were married. It bothered him that she looked so frail and tired.

She had surprised him a little by agreeing. "All right. It is a long drive back."

He'd put them up in the compact spare room of his trailer and then lay awake long into the night listening to the furnace kick on and off as the temperature dropped, wondering how in hell he was going to raise a child alone.

Harm must have taken his prolonged silence as a sign their conversation was at an end. He stood up, a short man, slightly stooped from years of manual labor but still strong, and began to pour water from a bucket he kept by the fire over the red-gold coals. Steam lifted into the cold air to mingle with the curling fingers of mist lying just above the surface of the lake. The cat reappeared at his feet and twined around his ankles, waiting to be let inside for the night. Harm stopped what he was doing and looked at Nate, his eyes narrowed against the smoke from the drowned embers. "You'll do right by the boy," he said. "I don't doubt that. But are you doing right by yourself taking her back?"

"SARAH. IT IS YOU. My dad said you were here but I just couldn't believe he wasn't mistaken." Arlene Fowler's words were as blunt as ever. She looked exactly as Sarah remembered her, too. She was a woman of medium height, a little overweight, but not fat. She had a pair of reading glasses pushed into the haphazard knot of hair on top of her head, glasses that she hadn't needed the last time Sarah had seen her. There was still very little gray in her light brown hair, and only a few laugh lines at the corners of her eyes and mouth, although she would have turned fifty-seven on her last birthday.

Arlene wasn't alone. She had a little girl with her. The child was wearing a pink satin windbreaker with "Barbie" stenciled on the front. She carried one of the dolls, frizzy-haired and naked, in each hand. Her little jeans had flared legs and her running shoes flashed hot pink lights along the side with each bouncing step. Her red-gold hair and turquoise-blue eyes matched Tessa's, Nate's youngest sister.

"Hello, Arlene." Sarah wished she didn't have to face Nate's mother alone, but she'd given up putting stock in wishes a long time ago.

"Is Nate here?"

"No." They had planned to see Arlene and his father, Tom, together as soon as Matty finished his breakfast. But that had obviously been too long for Nate's mother to wait. "He's in his workshop. He had to check on an overnight delivery of parts for the motorcycle he's restoring." It seemed odd that Nate had an ordinary job, and an ordinary life now. She had only known him as a soldier, a man with a dangerous MOS—military occupational specialty—performed under hazardous conditions, in war zones half a world away from those he loved.

"What are you doing here, Sarah?" Arlene's tone was brusque but there was an undertone of hurt and confusion in her question. "We haven't heard a word from you for over four years. Now you show up out of nowhere." The little girl leaned back against Arlene and bounced up and down on her toes, her crystal blue eyes fixed on Sarah like laser beams.

"Nate and I were coming to talk to you and Tom later this morning."

"I saved you the trip." Arlene's mouth thinned into a straight line. The momentary vulnerability Sarah had glimpsed in the older woman's eyes disappeared.

Sarah hadn't expected this to be easy. She liked Arlene. When things were good between her and Nate, she had felt they were on the road to becoming friends. But when they separated, Arlene had withdrawn her friendship. Sarah had hurt one of Arlene's own. That betrayal would not be easily forgiven.

"Mommy!" She looked down to see her son tugging on the leg of her jeans. He was wearing his Spider-Man pajamas that she'd bought for him for his birthday. He was growing so fast they were already an inch too short in the sleeves. He rubbed his eyes and grinned up at her.

"Hi, baby." She knelt down to give him a hug. If she didn't make it through the surgery she would consider herself in heaven if she could take the memory of that smile with her into the hereafter.

Arlene's little granddaughter quit jumping and stared at Matthew with her head tilted to one side. "Who are you?" she asked in a clear piping voice. "What are you doing in Unca' Nate's house?"

"Hush, Becca. Is this your son?" Arlene asked.

"Yes. This is Matthew. Matty, this is Mrs. Fowler. Nate's mother."

"My father said you had a child with you." She smiled as she shifted her gaze to the little boy. "Hello, Matty. My name is Arlene." Sarah relaxed. She should have known that Arlene wouldn't let whatever animosity she might still feel toward her spill over onto an innocent child. "This is my granddaughter, Rebecca."

"Hello." Shyness overcame him. He hid his face against Sarah's thigh.

Arlene's charge had no such problem. "I'm Becca. Who are you?"

Sarah gave Matty a little nudge. One eye peeped out. "Matthew David Taylor. I'm three years old." Matthew enunciated each word loudly and clearly.

"Me, too." Becca dropped the Barbies she was carrying and held up three chubby fingers on each hand.

"She's Tessa's, isn't she?" Sarah smiled down at the little girl. She would have liked a daughter someday, to dress in pink satin.

Arlene smiled, too. It was instantaneous and genuine, and reminded Sarah once more how fiercely devoted to her children Nate's mother was.

"Yes. She's expecting another at New Year's. A boy."

"I'm glad for her."

"I want toast," Matty announced.

"Yea, toast," Becca chimed, as she bent over to retrieve her dollies.

"Becca, you had breakfast already. Twice. Once with your mom and once more with me and Grandpa Tom." Arlene smoothed her hand indulgently over Becca's fine, flyaway curls as she spoke.

"Still hungry," Becca insisted.

"Why don't you come in and wait for Nate," Sarah offered, stepping back from the open door, then wished she hadn't when she saw Arlene's smile disappear. The words and gesture must have seemed too much like an invitation to a home that wasn't her own. "I...I'm sure he'll be back in a few minutes."

"I'm here now," Nate said coming up onto the deck that served as his front porch. It was roomy, stained silvery-gray to match the outside of the mobile home. The color scheme inside was predominately gray, too. Nate had painted all the paneling a creamy white above, and charcoal below. The carpet was the color of smoke, as was the overstuffed sofa and recliner that, along with a couple of lamps and tables and a big-screen TV, were the only furniture in the living room. The kitchen appliances were stainless steel, the countertops faux black granite. Even the built-in banquette, whose back contained open shelving that separated the living and kitchen areas, was upholstered in gray vinyl.

Those shelves were mostly empty, Sarah had noticed right away. There weren't any knickknacks on the tables or pictures on the walls. Nate had never liked clutter, she remembered. She, on the other hand, loved light and color, and liked to cover every surface with all manner of odd or pretty things she picked up at flea markets and yard sales. They used

to argue over her pack-rat tendencies, but like everything they had fallen out about, they'd always ended
their disagreement by making up and making love.
The strength and clarity of the memory caught her
by surprise. She hadn't thought about sex in months
and months. Had figured she would never think
about it again, but apparently she'd been wrong.

"Nate, what's this all about?" Arlene's voice demanded attention. "What's she doing here? What's
going on?"

NATE SAW the stricken look on Sarah's face and knew
the reason for it. The old saw about little pitchers
having big ears might be a cliché, but it was also right
on the money. Matty and Becca were staring at the
adults with intense interest.

"Hey, Becca Boo Jones. What are you doing
here?"

She held out her arms, a naked Barbie in each
hand. "Hi, Unca Nate."

"Aren't your dollies cold?" Nate knew the dolls
had clothes. He'd spent a ridiculous amount of
money outfitting one for Becca's birthday last spring.
He dropped stiffly to one knee wincing at the pain
in his bad ankle. She gave him a big hug, poking him
in the ribs with Barbie arms, squinching up her face
with the effort.

"Whoa," he said. "That's a good one."

"I want toast." She loosened her grip a little. "So does that boy." Her tone dripped with suspicion. She pointed a Barbie in Matty's direction. "Why's he here?"

"He and Sarah are staying with me for awhile. Sarah, would you make Becca and Matty some toast while I explain what's happening to Mom?"

Sarah gave him a grateful look. "C'mon, Becca. Do you like jelly on your toast?"

"No," Becca said firmly. "Cin'mon sweetie."

"She means cinnamon sugar. There's a shaker of the stuff in the first cupboard on the left. I keep it especially for this little monster." Nate gave Becca a gentle little push. "Go on inside. You're letting out all the warm air."

Becca hesitated. "Where are you going, Grandma?" she asked.

"Just to the barn...to look at the motorcycle. We'll be back before you're done eating your toast."

"Okay." She stood nose to nose with Sarah's son. "You want to play with me?"

Matty eyed the dolls with disapproval. "Not with dolls," he said with disdain. "Where's their clothes? It's cold outside."

"My dog ate them," Becca said. "And then he throwed them up. My mom throwed up, too, when she had to clean up the mess. She's going to have a baby. A boy. Right after Santa Claus comes. Right, Grandma?"

"New Year's Day," Arlene confirmed.

"That's nice." Sarah put her hand on Becca's shoulder and urged her inside.

"I'd rather have a sister," Becca said as the door closed behind them.

"What's going on, Nate?" Arlene asked, turning to face him. She made no move to leave the deck. She pushed her hands into the pocket of her fleece jacket and waited.

"We were coming over this morning to tell you and Dad about the situation." Arlene had her own insurance business with an office off the kitchen of the house he'd grown up in. Her hours were flexible so she was sometimes available for spur-of-the-moment babysitting for Becca, or his other sister Joann's two boys. His younger brother, Brandon, was in graduate school out of state, and in no hurry to add more leaves to the family tree.

"Situation? I don't like the sound of that. Anyway, your dad's at the doctor. He's getting some blood tests done." Tom Fowler was a Vietnam vet and a man of solid values and modest aspirations. He worked at a plant across the state line in Ohio that manufactured knock-down furniture. He was shift foreman now and counting the days until his retirement.

"Cholesterol up again?"

"Yes, but don't try and change the subject. Your

dad's blood tests are beside the point. Tell me what all this is about." There was a note of pleading in his mother's voice. It surprised him. Arlene Fowler tended to demand rather than plead.

Nate cleared his throat. "Sarah and I are getting married again."

"Married?" She sagged against the deck railing. "Oh, Lord. Nate, have you lost your senses? You haven't seen or spoken to each other for four years. And she has a child." She blinked hard. "Another man's child—"

Nate didn't want to hear that phrase again. "Sarah's very ill. She may be dying."

She stared at him for a moment with her mouth open in shock. "Dying? Are you sure?"

"I talked to her doctor yesterday." He leaned his hands on the railing and stared out over the lake as he told his mother everything that had happened in the last thirty-six hours. He wasn't sure he had all the medical terms right but he did his best to explain. The doctor hadn't been as pessimistic as Sarah that she wouldn't survive the surgery, but the prognosis hadn't been encouraging. "There's no way to know for certain without cutting her open if the growth has progressed beyond the point of no return."

"I…I had no idea." Arlene fumbled in the pockets of her coat, looking for the cigarettes she'd given up over a year ago. "But Nate, surely there's some other way? The boy's father?"

"Dead," he said flatly.

"Oh, Lord. I'm sorry. I didn't know—"

"How could you?"

"No, I guess I couldn't know. I'm ashamed to say I never answered her last couple of letters, or made any effort to stay in touch." She lifted her hands in a helpless little gesture. "That can't be changed now. I…I have to admit I've wondered off and on how she was doing the last couple of years, but I never suspected anything like this. How long has she been widowed?"

"Since before Matty was born."

"And her husband had no family, either?"

"None that can help her. She's as alone in the world as she ever was. That's why I've agreed to take responsibility for Matty."

"Oh, Nate." Arlene covered her mouth with her hand for a moment. "I know how much you used to love her, but to do this for a woman who broke your heart."

"What happened between Sarah and me is in the past. It's about what's best for the boy now."

"A child who isn't yours—"

"Mom. It's settled." She winced at the hardness he couldn't keep out of his voice.

In silence they watched as Harm came out of his

cabin and moved slowly down toward the lakeshore, tackle box in hand, followed by Buster. The old man was probably heading out to try and catch a mess of late-season pan fish for his supper; it was anyone's guess where the cat was headed. The growl of Harm's old Evinrude outboard motor broke the morning quiet.

"When?" Arlene asked after a few moments.

"We can pick up the license Friday afternoon. Mayor Holder, over at Lakeview, has us penciled in for five o'clock that afternoon. Sarah's surgery is scheduled for seven a.m. Saturday morning."

"So soon?" Impulsively his mother reached out and laid her hand over his. He turned his palm up and closed his hand around her cold fingers.

"It has to be, Mom. I can't let Matty grow up the way Sarah did, shuffled from one foster home to the next, no security, no place to put down roots. He needs stability and a family. I'll do my best to give him that."

"When you put it that way I suppose there's no use me arguing with you. You've always been the most stubborn of my kids, and that's saying something. Always trying to get the rest of the world to march to your drummer." She gave his hand a hard squeeze then fumbled in her coat pocket for a tissue.

"Don't you think I'm up to the challenge?"

"Of course you are. You'll make a wonderful father! Maybe this is the Almighty's way of giving you—"

He knew where she was going with that line of thought and was glad that she stopped herself so he didn't have to.

"God, I wish I had a cigarette," she said, dabbing at her eyes with a tissue.

"You haven't had a smoke for over a year. Don't go backsliding now."

"Easy for you to say," she sniffed. "Do I look okay?"

"You look fine."

"I'm so glad I didn't launch into Sarah with both barrels. Or you, for that matter. Two whole days of wondering what she was doing here. Your father warned me not—"

"Will you tell him, Mom? It would save me some time."

"I'll tell him," she blew out a puff of breath. "He always liked Sarah but I don't think he's going to be any happier about this than I am."

"You don't have to be happy about it. Just stand by me."

"Till my last breath," she said fiercely. "Let's go inside. I suppose I should get to know Matty a little better so he won't be afraid to stay with me while…while Sarah is in the hospital."

"Thanks, Mom." Nate bent his head to give her a peck on the cheek. She wrapped her arms around him and gave him a quick, hard hug.

"I know you think you're doing the right thing,

and I suppose you are. But, oh Nate, she hurt you so badly."

"We hurt each other, Mom, but that's not what's important now. She came to me as a last resort. There's nothing left between us but a little boy who needs our love."

She put her hand on his forearm as he turned to go back inside. "Nate, I just thought of something. What if the doctors are wrong? What if the surgery is a success? If Sarah is granted her miracle, what will you do then?"

CHAPTER THREE

HER WEDDING DAY was over.

In a few hours they would leave for the hospital. The trailer was quiet so Nate must have fallen asleep at last. The walls of the mobile home were thin and she had heard him tossing long into the night. It hadn't always been that way. When they were married—before—he had always slept like a log, barely moving from the position in which he fell asleep. *Always with her snuggled tight against him, safe and protected in his arms.*

Best to stay away from memories like that.

It was why she dreaded the small hours of the night—the barriers she kept strong and in good repair during the day failed her in the darkness. The week had passed quickly. There had been lawyer's visits, small domestic chores, precious time spent with Matty as he played with Becca and became more at ease with Nate and his family. But the nights had been long and stressful, for both of them.

She glanced around the shadowed room. All of

Matty's things were arranged to his satisfaction. His favorite SpongeBob SquarePants lamp was on top of the dresser. His clothes were folded in the drawers and hanging in the little closet next to hers, his toys piled into a new bright yellow storage unit in the corner. The fireproof box with all the documentation Nate would need when he became responsible for her son was sitting on Nate's dresser.

She had sold or given away most of her possessions except for those she could pack in the minivan. Still, it had been difficult to find room for all of it in Nate's trailer. There simply wasn't much storage space. Matty's baby book, the albums with pictures of his father and his Taylor relatives, were stored on the top shelf of the closet along with the few photographs various sets of foster parents had taken of her over the years. There was also the video of her when she was pregnant that David had made, which ended when she was seven months along, and he died. Later, she had taken some footage of Matty when he was small to add to it, but her heart was never in it and she'd ended up selling the video camera to one of her co-workers at HomeContractors so she could buy a still camera.

She was a throwback, she guessed. She loved photographs, the kind you could hold in your hand, put in an album to linger over, savor, relive. She had taken roll after roll of film of her son, a set for each year of his life. The camera was in the safe box, too. She hoped someday Matty would want to learn to use it when he was old enough.

There were no pictures of her and Nate among the keepsakes, however. She had destroyed them the day their divorce became final.

And there had been no pictures taken today, although she suspected Tessa had a camera in her car. She and her husband, Keith, a long-distance trucker, had acted as their witnesses for the short, informal ceremony in the mayor's office at the back of the red-brick building that housed Lakeview's six-man police force, as well as its municipal offices. There had been no rice to throw, no cake to cut. And no toasts to a long and happy life together. Because there wouldn't be one.

Their whirlwind remarriage was probably already the talk of the entire population around Cottonwood Lake. More than once Sarah had caught the mayor taking in every detail of her simple navy blue dress and Nate's dark suit. There had been an absence of flowers, except for the nosegay of fall mums that Arlene had pressed into her hands when they dropped Matty off at her house—all brides need a bouquet she'd said, shrugging off Sarah's thanks. And the lack of other family and friends in attendance, and that no further celebration appeared planned to mark the event, was all grist for the gossip mill of a very small town. It was Nate who remembered the ring, a simple gold band that fit perfectly but felt heavy and unfamiliar on her hand. And a kiss, light and soft and warm as sunshine on her mouth. Another memory that wouldn't go away.

A shadow blocked the light from the hallway. She turned her head to see Nate's broad shoulders filling the narrow doorway. He was fully dressed except for his shoes. He was wearing jeans and a gray chamois shirt, open at the throat, the sleeves rolled up to just below his elbows. He braced one shoulder against the door frame and pushed his hand into the front pocket of his jeans. The casual, masculine clothes suited him, just as his Army uniform had. She could never picture Nate wearing a suit every day, or working behind a desk, an office-bound, cubicle-dweller chained to a keyboard and monitor. He was a man born to be outside, to work with his hands.

"You should be asleep," he said quietly.

"I'm not sleepy."

"The doctor said you should get all the rest you can."

"I'll have eternity to rest." She smoothed the blanket over Matty's knees. She was tired and scared and her emotions were too close to the surface to easily control. "I'm sorry. I didn't mean to sound melodramatic."

"You shouldn't dwell on the worst-case scenario."

"You always dwell on the worst-case scenario when you're a single parent."

There was a heartbeat's silence before he answered. "You're not a single parent anymore, remember."

"No, I'm not. Not anymore," she whispered.

Matty frowned in his sleep, then he raised his little fists and rubbed his eyes. "Mommy," he called, sitting up, looking around with an unfocused stare. He began to sob, caught up in a bad dream.

"Shhh, baby," she crooned, pulling him close. "I'm right here."

Sarah didn't need a child psychologist to tell her why Matty was suddenly having nightmares. His whole world had been turned upside down. He didn't understand the gravity of her condition, at least she prayed he didn't, but he knew something was wrong and the uncertainty of his new life scared him.

"He goes right back to sleep if you rock him," she whispered to Nate. Matty had stuck his thumb in his mouth as he snuggled tight against her. "Just take his thumb out of his mouth when you put him back down." She heard the quaver in her voice and fell silent.

"I'll remember," Nate said, and the words sounded like a promise. "Do you want me to hold him?"

She shook her head. She knew his suggestion

made sense, but she couldn't let go of her baby. Not now, not even for a little while. There were so many things to teach Nate about Matty but she couldn't trust her voice any longer. "I need to hold him."

"Why don't you try to sleep? I'll wake you at four. Mom will be here to watch over him so we can leave by four-forty-five." Her surgery was scheduled for seven but they needed to check into the hospital an hour earlier.

"All right." She laid Matty down on his pillow and curled up beside him. She closed her arms around him and felt the quick, light beat of his heart against hers.

Nate stepped into the room and pulled the sheet over them both. He didn't say anything more, urge her to sleep, or wish her pleasant dreams. It would have been a waste of breath. But she thought she felt the merest brush of his fingers in her hair, and then he was gone and she was alone with her son in her arms.

IT HAD BEEN the longest day of his life and that included those he'd spent in battle, Nate thought, watching the last of the orange and gray sunset fade from the night sky. He turned away from the window. He and his parents were alone in the waiting room.

It was small and tucked away at the end of a long hall.

The kind of room they put you in to give you bad news.

"What time is it?" Arlene asked, looking up from the magazine she'd been pretending to read for the last half hour.

"Almost six," Tom responded. Nate had thought his father was asleep he'd been quiet for so long, his long legs crossed at the ankles, his chin resting on his chest, as he sat slouched in a brown tweed chair.

His parents had shown up at the hospital about an hour after Sarah's surgery had started. "I know I promised Sarah we'd watch look after Matty," Arlene told him with the stubborn look on her face that all of her children had learned at an early age not to argue with. "He'll do fine with Joann and the boys. You need us more than he does right now." They hadn't left his side for a moment since.

"Only six o'clock and it's dark already," Arlene sighed.

"It'll be dark even earlier when daylight savings time ends." Tom straightened from his slouched position and stretched his arms over his head. He was a couple of inches taller than Nate, although they favored each other in looks.

Arlene dropped the magazine and stood up, walking to the door and looking out into the hallway. "How much longer do you think it will be?"

Nate shrugged. "Six to eight hours. That's what the surgeon said."

"And the surgery started at noon?"

"Yes," he answered patiently. It was the third time she'd asked.

He and Sarah had arrived at the pre-op suite right at six. But from then on nothing had gone as planned. The doctor was in surgery, an emergency, an apologetic nurse had informed them. Sarah's operation had been moved back on the schedule. There was a room they could wait in, she'd explained, while Sarah filled out forms. She knew what Sarah was facing and she did her best to put them at ease.

Later another nurse had taken Sarah away to undress and change into a hospital gown, leaving him to cool his heels in the windowless cubbyhole of a room. He stared at the gauges and tubing affixed to the wall above the empty space where Sarah's bed would be. Oxygen, blood pressure cuff, monitors that he couldn't read. He switched his gaze to the TV and pretended to watch the early morning weather report. A few minutes later they brought Sarah in. She looked small and lost in the high bed with its stark white sheets and pillowcase. She wore a worn-looking white surgical gown and her hair was hidden beneath a paper cap.

"They didn't shave my head if that's what you're wondering," she said with a ghost of the smile that still had the power to make his heart beat harder. "The incision will be here." She touched the back of her neck.

The nurse started an IV and gave Sarah the first of her pre-op medication. A few minutes later she seemed to doze off. Nate stared at the TV and the clock, not paying attention to the one and wondering if the other was broken since the hands didn't seem to move. Nurses came and went with more medication for the IV. Sarah woke up and turned her head to look at him. "I forgot to tell you," she said, swallowing against the dryness in her mouth. They'd probably given her atropine to do that. Nate knew more about pre-op medications than he wanted to. "Matty wants to be Shrek for Halloween. He's excited about it. Do you think you can find a costume for him?"

Nate stood up and walked over to the high bed. He leaned both hands on the rails the nurse had put up when she started the IV. "I'll make sure he has a Shrek costume," he promised.

The answer seemed to please her. A faint smile curved her mouth and her words took on a dreamy tone. "Spoken like a true father. See, I told you you'd be good at the daddy thing. Thank you, Nate. For everything."

He'd reached down to take her hand in his at the same moment the surgeon appeared in the doorway. She was young, with chocolate-colored skin, a serious demeanor, and an excellent reputation in her field. "It's time to go," she'd said.

Sarah's fingers tightened around his. "Try to learn to love him, Nate. That's all I ask."

His last words to her were spoken directly from his heart. "I won't have to try at all."

"Someone's coming." Arlene's voice broke into his thoughts. She took a couple of steps backward into the waiting room and turned to face him. "Is Sarah's doctor a very pretty, young black woman?"

"Yes. Dr. Jamison." He curled his hands around the back of one of the brown tweed chairs so his parents couldn't see them tremble.

Tom rose, too, as the neurosurgeon entered the room. She was wearing rose-colored scrubs and green surgical booties, her short, dark hair still covered by a white paper cap like the one they'd put on Sarah. She carried a clipboard and a large envelope in her hands, looking down at her notes as she walked. Nate searched her face for signs of the bad news he was certain she'd come to deliver. She looked up and saw them watching her, and smiled.

Not the polite curve of her generous mouth that Nate had seen earlier, but a real smile that reached her eyes and banished the weariness from her face. "I've got good news," she said. Nate had been preparing himself for the worst, and if he hadn't been watching her so closely he would have thought he'd heard her wrong. "The surgery was a complete success. Sarah is going to be just fine."

"A miracle," Arlene whispered, and sat down in her chair with a thump, as though her legs would no longer support her. Nate felt weak in the knees himself.

"Well, not exactly a miracle, but very close to one." Dr. Jamison pulled a sheet of X rays out of the envelope and snapped them into the light box on the wall by the door. "These are your wife's pre-op scans." She pointed to a spidery web of lines curled over and around the vertebrae of Sarah's neck and then indicated the second X ray, where there were no more lines. "The growth was advancing very rapidly. Another few millimeters, and it would have been too late." She stared at the scans for a moment with a satisfied smile, then snapped off the light. "But we don't have to go there anymore. It was touch and go for awhile, but I think I can safely assure you the chance of a recurrence is less than five percent over the next—" her smile grew a little wider "—fifty years or so."

Nate felt as if a bomb had at last gone off in his face. Blood roared in his ears and for a minute he forgot to breathe. She was going to be all right. *And she was his wife again.* How were they going to deal with that? Automatically, he held out his hand. "Thank you for everything, Doctor."

"I'm so pleased to be able to give you such a good prognosis. I don't have to tell you I didn't think the outcome would be so favorable." She glanced down at Arlene, who was staring up at her. "Maybe your mother is right. Maybe there was a little bit of a miracle worked in the mix."

"A miracle," Arlene repeated, turning her eyes to Nate.

"Sarah should make a complete recovery over the next couple of months, Mr. Fowler. She'll need some therapy for the nerve damage to her arm and leg, but I believe it's completely reversible. The therapy will all be out-patient, of course. Barring any unforeseen complications you can take her home in seventy-two hours."

"Is there anything I can get for you?"

"No, thank you." At the last moment the constriction of the brace around her neck reminded her not to try and shake her head. "I'm fine. Just a little tired. Matty—?"

"He's with Tessa, remember."

"Oh, yes, of course. I…I forgot." She missed Matty terribly. She'd never been away from him this long before, although in reality it had only been four days. Ninety-six hours that had changed her world.

"It's normal. The anesthetic, the pain medication. Your brain won't feel like such a block of wood after you get some sleep." Nate wasn't looking at her as he spoke, but was hanging their coats in the postage-stamp-size closet beside the door.

"I imagine you're right." He was talking from experience, she reminded herself. How many surgeries had he undergone to reconstruct his knee and ankle? It hadn't been a subject that had come up during the few days they'd been together before the wedding. Odd, not to know something that at one point in her life would have been of the utmost significance. Even now she couldn't bear to think of him hurting and in pain. Her palm itched, so she absently rubbed the tips of her fingers over the skin. It was another sign the surgery had been successful, this uncomfortable, almost annoying return of sensation to her nerve-deadened hand and leg. She kept her eyes on the lake. Gray clouds scudded overhead changing the surface of the water from blue to pewter as swiftly as her moods seemed to swing between light and dark, happiness at being alive and near despair at the dilemma she'd created for Nate and herself.

She had been prepared to die.

Not to live.

She had believed wholeheartedly that she wouldn't survive the surgery. She'd made him believe it, too, or he wouldn't have agreed to her mad scheme. But she had survived. Yet in her fear and anxiety to provide for her son what had she done?

To Nate?

To the two of them?

The thought made her head swim. Her knees felt weak and rubbery. She put her hand out to steady herself on the arm of Nate's huge recliner. It was a man's chair, wide and overstuffed. David had had one much like it. She'd sold it along with all her other furniture before she left Texas.

Immediately Nate was at her side, helping to lower her gingerly onto the seat. She steeled herself not to jerk away from his touch. To have him so close made her wary of her reactions. He was so big and warm and safe. It would be wonderful to give in to the temptation of being taken care of again. But she didn't dare allow herself the luxury of such yearnings for even a moment. She and Matty were on their own, or would be again soon enough. "Thanks," she said, "wobbly knees."

"Your blood sugar's probably low. I'll make you some tea and toast. Then you can get some rest."

"Please, don't bother. I'm fine. I ate everything on my tray before we left the hospital." And the food, bland as it was, was still sitting like lead in her queasy stomach.

Unheeding of her words, he moved into the small kitchen. Nate was a good cook, she remembered. All the men in his family were—it was a competition of sorts between them at holidays and parties. "While you're resting I'll go down to the barn and check the answering machine before I head over to Tessa's and bring Matty home."

Bring Matty home. Another of the phrases that sounded so right but was so wrong.

"We need to talk—" she repeated stubbornly.

"I've put you two in the bigger bedroom." He spoke over his shoulder. "There's more room for your things. Matty helped me move your stuff."

"We can't force you out of your bedroom."

"I'm fine in the small room. I think I'll have a cup of coffee before I go to the barn. Are you sure you don't want something? Tea? Cocoa? I make great cocoa."

"So Becca told me." She wished her head didn't feel like the block of wood Nate had described, but it did. She'd gotten little sleep in the busy teaching hospital the past three nights. She was so tired that she couldn't keep a clear line of thought in her head. The pain-killers she'd taken before she checked out of the hospital weren't helping her concentration, either. But the truth was she needed them, at least for the time being.

"You know, cocoa sounds good now that I think of it. I'll make us both a cup." He opened the refrigerator and pulled out a gallon of milk and filled a saucepan on the stove with the deliberate, efficient movements and total concentration on the task at hand that Sarah remembered from their time together. That way of working, of moving, had been drilled into him in the military. When you dealt with explosives, impatience and carelessness were two traits guaranteed to get you, or someone else, killed. He'd told her that early in their relationship when they'd had no trouble talking about what was important to them.

He reached one long arm across the narrow counter and took a tin of cocoa and sugar from a top cupboard shelf in one smooth, unhurried motion. *He made love the same way, deliberately and thoroughly.* Sarah pushed herself out of the big chair and walked slowly to the banquette. She sat down then removed the neck brace and placed it on the seat beside her. She only needed to wear it when she was riding in the car or walking outside, where her weakened leg muscles might trip her up. She gingerly touched the back of her neck where the row of metal staples held the edges of the long incision together. In ten days they would be removed, and the small amount of her hair that had been shaved away would grow back almost as quickly, Dr. Jamison had assured her. After that it would be therapy twice a week for six weeks at Lakeview Care Manor across the lake, and then a follow-up visit to Dr. Jamison. If everything looked good she would be allowed to drive and go back to work in time for the holiday rush.

She would start apartment hunting then, and she and Matty could be in their own place by Christmas. Except she would still be married to Nate. She rested her head in her hands. It was all so complicated now. The financial arrangements she'd made were predicated on her death, not her living. She had very little ready cash. On top of everything else he had done for her, would she end up having to ask Nate for a loan to divorce him again?

Lord, what a mess. Her head was pounding; the incision ached. She was so tired she could barely keep her eyes open, yet she was too restless to sleep. Nate set a cup of cocoa in front of her. It smelled so delicious she opened her eyes and picked up the mug, savoring the warmth of the china, grateful for her renewed ability to correctly judge the degree of heat against her skin.

"Eat," Nate urged.

Obediently she ate a triangle of toast, then another. Before she knew it the plate was empty. She said the first thing that came to her mind. "Toast and cocoa. Your mother's remedy for whatever ails you."

"Looks like it hasn't lost its effectiveness. Want some more?"

"No, thank you. That was enough."

"Then I'll turn down the bed for you."

"No." The word came out louder than she'd planned.

"If you feel that strongly about it you can turn down the bed yourself." He leaned back against the counter smiling slightly, indulgently.

"I don't need a nap. We have to talk. Now." She wasn't going to let him steamroller over her the way he sometimes had before.

"All right, we'll talk if that's what you want. Go ahead." Frowning, he folded his arms over his chest.

"We need to figure how to get ourselves out of this mess I've gotten us into."

"We don't need to do that right this minute."

"Yes, we do." Sarah stopped and took a deep breath. "Please, sit down. It hurts when I have to look up at you."

He did as she asked, resting his arms on the tabletop. His forearms were dusted with dark hairs, his wrists and hands were strong, the muscles and tendons taut beneath his skin. "Go on, say what's on your mind."

"Our marriage is what's on my mind. It will all have to be undone. We'll have to contact the lawyer again, explain the situation. He's probably waiting to hear from you so he can read my will."

"You have a point. We should call his office and tell him you came through the surgery with flying colors. The rest of it can wait until you're back on your feet."

The next words were harder to say. "I—I'll probably have to ask you for a loan to pay my share. And for a security deposit on an apartment. I'll borrow against my life insurance policy as soon as I can make the arrangements, but I canceled my credit card so I can't get an advance that way—"

He held up his hand. There was no longer any hint of a smile on his face or in his words. "Not so fast. Dr. Jamison said she'd let you return to work in six to eight weeks. That's if everything is okay. You're not going to be able to care for Matty by yourself for most of that time. How the hell do you think you're going to manage alone until then?"

"I'll find day care—"

He leaned back, once more folding his arms across his chest. "Good day care's expensive. But more importantly your son's been moved from pillar to post and back again over the past couple of months. He's just getting used to my family. And me. There's no need to uproot him again. Not for the time being."

"I can't stay here, Nate."

Nate's gray eyes never left hers but they allowed her no access to his thoughts. "If you want I'll move in with Granddad for a couple of weeks so you two can have your own space. But not right away, not until you're up on your feet again. Matty's too much for you to handle alone."

He had a point there, one she could scarcely argue with. She wasn't allowed to lift anything over five pounds. Matty was a rambunctious three-year-old but he was still her baby. He needed help in and out of the bathtub, on and off the toilet. He wanted to be held and cuddled. She couldn't do any of those things for him, at least not without help.

Nate's help.

"I don't want to be taken care of, Nate. Not anymore." She had wanted exactly that once upon a time, and she had let herself slide too far into the fairy tale. Then when she tried to assert herself by insisting on a baby when he was afraid to give her one, the conflict had shattered their make-believe world, and their marriage.

His face darkened. He stood and picked up her plate and cup, turning his back as he set the dirty dishes in the sink. "I know that, Sarah. You pretty much burned it into my brain when we divorced. But the long and short of it is right now you do need someone to take care of you. And that someone is me."

What a mess she'd made of things. "I'm sorry, Nate," she whispered. Her hands trembled and fatigue washed over her in a black wave. She fought to keep her concentration focused on their discussion, but all she really wanted to do was go to sleep.

"There's nothing to be sorry for. We got a miracle handed to us. We can't complain because it's got strings attached." He turned to look at her again, leaning his hip against the sink. The darkness was gone from his face, if not from his gray eyes. "I admit we've got a boatload of problems to work out, but outside of calling the lawyer with the good news none of them have to be dealt with today. You've only been out of the hospital for two hours. Go rest. I'll get Matty from Tessa's and wake you when I bring him back. We'll form a plan of attack tomorrow."

"You make it sound as if you're staging a war game."

He shook his head, smiling ruefully. "Yeah, I guess I do. Old habits die hard."

That wasn't all, Sarah thought as she curled herself around the oversize pillow that Dr. Jamison had recommended she use so that she didn't lie on her back and put pressure on the incision. Old dreams died hard, too.

CHAPTER FOUR

NATE STARED at his reflection in the rechromed head-light of the Indian as he wiped a smudged fingerprint off the shiny surface. He looked like hell. He hoped it was only from the distortion of the metal and not evidence of another week of sleepless nights. He'd always prided himself on being able to sleep through anything, including mortar attacks, and the midnight shift change in a busy military hospital. But he was wrong. He'd found something that could keep him awake for hours, even though it was no louder than the sound of someone breathing. Sarah's breathing, soft and even, in the room just down the hall.

He'd probably get more sleep if he bunked down out here on the lumpy old futon Joann had foisted on him after her last garage sale.

Hell, why was he thinking of bedtime? The sun wasn't even down yet.

He looked at his watch. "Damn." He was sup-posed to pick Matty up half an hour ago, but he'd been so focused on the restoration he'd lost track of time. Some kind of father he was turning out to be. He grabbed a jacket and headed out the door just as his sisters and their assorted offspring tumbled out of Tessa's van.

Or to be more precise, the kids tumbled out of the van. Ty, Joann's almost-nine-year-old, turned back to help unfasten Becca from her car seat while Matty, already released from his safety seat, raced across the parking lot only a step or two behind seven-year-old Jack. Joann strolled along in the kids' wake while Tessa and her impressive belly brought up the rear. Both of his sisters were tall women with round, pretty features. Joann was blond and built along the same generous lines as their mother while Tessa, when she wasn't pregnant, had the thinner build and red-gold hair that came from the Fowler side of the family.

"Hi, Nate." Jack and Matty came skidding to a halt in front of him. "Can we see the bike? Is it done? Can I ride it yet?"

"No, it isn't done. But I've got the gas tank back on, and the handlebars. It's beginning to look like a real bike again. Go ahead, take a look. But don't try to climb up on it." Jack had been clambering on anything that would hold still, and a few things that wouldn't, since he was about six months old.

His nephew made a face. "I know better than that," he said, but his eyes didn't quite meet Nate's, so Nate knew he'd been planning to do exactly that.

"C'mon, Matty. Let's go."

Matty held back. "I want to see my mom." He looked up at Nate with hopeful eyes.

"She's taking a nap," Nate informed him. "We'll go wake her up in just a little while. Where'd you get that hat?" It was a navy blue ball cap with a big gold block *M* on the front.

"From Jack."

"My dad said Matty needed to get with the program so I gave him my hat. It's too little for me anyway." Gus Westin, Joann's husband, was the science teacher at the local junior high, and a former third-string kicker for Michigan. Jack was the spitting image of his father—dark-haired, small-boned and wiry tough. He wasn't all that much bigger than Sarah's son and still young enough to play with Matty so they got along well.

Nate patted Matty on top of the head. "Looks good on you, buddy."

Matty reached up and pulled on the brim. "I like it."

"Let's go," Jack urged. Dark-haired Ty, who had a leaner build than his brother, let go of Becca's hand and took Matty's.

"C'mon. I'll go with you."

"Keep your eye on him," Joann admonished her firstborn. "And your brother."

"I will." The three boys took off for the barn leaving Nate with the girls.

"Hi, Unca' Nate," Becca chirped. "We're going shopping, wanna come along?"

"Hi, Becca Boo." The little girl held up her arms to be lifted for a hug and a kiss. He found himself wishing that Matty would do the same, but so far the little boy hadn't initiated any hugs. Patience, he told himself, it had only been a couple of weeks—it took time to earn a kid's trust, especially a little one who'd had been through the kind of upheaval Matty had.

"I'm sorry, sis. I lost track of time." Nate directed his apology to Tessa, who had plunked herself down on the retaining wall that jutted out from the front corner of the barn, puffing slightly, her hand on her distended stomach.

"No, problem. We're just heading into Adrian to get some groceries and some more trick-or-treat candy." Adrian was the nearest large town.

"The boys found my hiding place," Joann explained with a shake of her head as Nate set Becca on the low stone wall beside her mother. "I'm going to put this batch in the safe-deposit box at the bank." Joann was the loan officer at a bank in Hillsdale, in the next county, and Nate had no doubt she'd be at least a vice president there one day.

"We can take Matty with us, if you'd like," Tessa offered after a slight hesitation and an exchange of glances with Joann. "I imagine Sarah's pretty worn-out."

Nate knew his sisters were genuinely happy that Sarah had survived the surgery, but he was also fully aware they had reservations, for his sake, not only about the remarriage, but also about Sarah remaining in his home. Tessa, who had been closest to Sarah in the past, would take her cue from him. Joann, like their mother, was not as softhearted, nor as easygoing. She had always liked Sarah, but she had also been more outspoken in her anger when they divorced. She was fiercely loyal to her family and Nate suspected it would take time for her to forgive and forget.

"That's okay. You guys have been lifesavers this past couple of weeks. He'll be fine with me. I'm sure Sarah will be waking up from her nap soon. You're right, she was exhausted after her therapy session."

"How's she doing?"

"Great. Nearly all the feeling's back in her hands and fingers. Her leg's coming along, too, just a little more slowly."

"Good," Tessa responded with a smile, and Joann nodded her agreement.

"Want us to bring you back takeout for dinner?"

"Thanks for offering, but I've got baked steak in the oven."

"With mashed potatoes and gravy?"

"Of course." He grinned as Joann rolled her eyes heavenward and sighed.

"Lord, I hate these low-carb diets. I'd give up my stock options for mashed potatoes and gravy!"

"Umm," Tessa seconded.

Nate did some quick figuring in his head. "You're welcome to stay. I think we can make it stretch if I stir up some macaroni and cheese for the kids."

Joann sighed again. "Thanks for offering but we promised the kids pizza, and I'm bound and determined to stick to this diet. I've gained five pounds in the last couple of weeks and I swear I haven't cheated once. It's the damned salad bar for me."

Nate grinned. "Man, that's hardship duty, sis. Watching those two eating machines, Ty and Jack, chow down on pizza while you're grazing through the spinach and sprouts."

"Hey, that's hitting below the belt." Joann made a face and stuck out her lower lip in a pout. "Just for that you can make your four-cheese, sour cream potato casserole with the crushed potato-chip topping for the pumpkin smashing party Saturday." Joann slapped her hand over her mouth. "Oohh, what made me say that? Now I'll be dreaming about the darned thing for the next three days."

The "Saturday After Halloween Jack-O-Lantern Smashing Party" was one of his sisters' newest "family traditions," the one they sandwiched between the Labor Day water-ski exhibition, and the chili cook-off that preceded the Ohio State/Michigan game the Saturday before Thanksgiving—when they really ratcheted up the entertaining schedule.

"You know, Joann," Tessa said slyly, wrapping her arms around Becca's shoulders and nuzzling the top of her head, "the last time you obsessed about potatoes you were pregnant with Jack."

"I did not."

"Yes, you did," Nate said, surprised that he remembered, babies and pregnancies never having been a high priority for him in the old days. "I was home on leave then." *Just weeks before he met Sarah.* "You ate them morning, noon and night. Boiled, fried, mashed, baked and raw. I remember thinking it was the weirdest pregnancy craving I'd ever heard of."

"It's impossible." Joann's eyes were big as saucers but she didn't sound quite as certain as she had before. "Gus and I haven't even thought about another baby. I mean not seriously." Her words drifted off into horrified silence. "There was that one night last month when the boys were sleeping over at Mom and Dad's and the con—" She colored and changed the subject. "No way," she said, then in a strangled voice, "What's the date?"

Tessa laughed and stood up, lifting Becca down off the wall. "It's the twenty-ninth. How late are you?"

Joann swallowed hard. "Not much, not really... Oh, hell..."

"Looks, like we need to add an EPT kit to the shopping list."

"It's not funny," Joann wailed. "I don't even keep track anymore. What's Gus going to say?" She blew her bangs back off her forehead. "I'm thirty three-years old. I'm too old for another baby. Maybe it's early menopause?"

"Don't be ridiculous," Tessa scolded. "You're way too young to be starting menopause. I think you're pregnant. It's something I can sense. You know, like calling to like." She pointed down at her bulging stomach. "And if you are pregnant, you'll be thrilled as soon as you get used to the idea. You know Gus has always wanted a little girl."

Becca had been taking it all in. Standing on tiptoe she reached up and patted Tessa's stomach. "I want a little girl, too."

"Our baby's a boy," Tessa explained patiently for what Nate guessed must be the hundredth time, while Joann fumbled through her coat pocket for a tissue.

"Jack will trade me for it," she pronounced, nodding so hard her pigtails bounced up and down. "You'll trade us babies won't you A'nt Joann."

"I'm not having a—" Joann stopped in midsentence. Looking past Nate's left shoulder she said, "Hello, Sarah."

"Hi, Joann. Tessa, hello." Sarah was making her

way carefully toward them. She wasn't wearing the neck brace anymore, although Nate wished she would when she walked on the uneven ground around the barn, but didn't say so. Sarah had made it clear enough over the last week that she wasn't going to play the invalid any longer than necessary.

"Hi, Sarah."

"Hi," Becca piped up. "Matty's in the barn."

"Is he? I'll have to go get him. I've been missing him." She slid her hands into the pockets of her light-weight cotton jacket and smiled tentatively at Joann and Tessa. "I hope I didn't interrupt anything."

"No, of course not. We were just checking to see if Nate needed anything from Wal-Mart. We're on our way there for a last minute trick-or-treat run."

"Do you have enough candy, Nate?" Sarah asked him. "I'd be happy to contribute some if Tessa and Joann could pick it up for me."

"I've got plenty. We're too far off the beaten track up here to get more than a few trick-or-treaters."

"Just turn off your porch light if you run out," Tessa suggested. "That's pretty much the universal signal for 'no candy.'"

"Got that, Sarah? Blackout conditions are to be put into effect when you run out of ammunition," Nate said with a grin. "I'm taking Matty out in his Shrek costume and Sarah's staying here to hold down the fort."

"I'm perfectly capable of taking Matty trick-or-treating."

"You might miss your footing in the dark," Tessa said. "You wouldn't want to take a tumble."

"That's why she's staying here and passing out candy." Nate heard his old sergeant's voice coming out of his mouth but he didn't care.

Sarah didn't challenge him as he half expected her to. Instead she changed the subject. "I want to thank you both for watching over Matty these last two weeks. I appreciate it very much."

"We're glad to help out," Joann said. "I'll go get the boys. We should be on our way." She hurried toward the workshop door without a backward glance.

"We really do need to be heading out," Tessa said to explain her sister's abrupt departure. "I want to stop and ask Grandpa if he needs anything on the way, and Ty has a spelling test to study for."

"Of course," Sarah said with another smile, but Nate could see Joann's coolness bothered her.

Thirty seconds later the boys came charging out of the barn followed by Matty and Nate's sister. "See, I told you she was right here," Joann said, giving him a little push forward.

"Mama." He wrapped both arms around Sarah's leg and held her tight. "I'm home."

"I see that. I missed you." She hugged him back.

"I got a new hat," he said, leaning back so that she could admire the ball cap. "Jack gave it to me."

"I like it."

"We'll see you Saturday," Tessa called over her shoulder. "We'll be over early to sweep the barn and set up the tables."

"Gus and his students will be here around three to unload the trebuchet," Joann reminded him. "I hope the rain holds off until after dark."

"It will," Nate said under his breath so that only Sarah could hear. "There isn't a rain cloud in this state that would dare unload on one of my sisters' parties."

"I've never heard of a trebuchet," Sarah said as they watched Tessa back the van around and head back down the hill to Harm's place. "What is it and what does it have to do with Halloween?"

"Absolutely nothing to do with Halloween. It's a medieval war machine. Kind of a cross between a catapult and a sling shot." Nate held open the door of the low-ceilinged workshop for her and Matty.

"Is that what they're called? They used them in the battle of Helm's Deep in *The Two Towers,*" Sarah said, with a grin. "I watched it the other day." She rested her left elbow on her right hand and made a flinging motion. "The bad guys were lobbing severed heads over the wall."

"The severed head lobbing was in *The Return of*

the King. The bad guys were using catapults. The good guys were flinging back huge pieces of stone. And *they* were using trebuchets."

"I'll have to watch the whole thing again to get it straight in my head. Did your sisters get the idea for the pumpkin smashing party from the movies?"

"I don't think so. It's been going on since Gus's science club built the darn thing and they needed ammunition that was cheap and that wouldn't cause fatal injuries. Joann suggested jack-o'-lanterns after she read about some place back east that does it every year with intact pumpkins, and the rest is Riley's Cove history."

"Sounds like fun. Your sisters are good at things like that. I remember the Fourth of July celebration when you were home on leave the summer after we were married. Toasted marshmallows, hot dogs and potato salad, homemade ice cream—the whole nine yards. And the fireworks were great. I'd never been to a party like that before." There wasn't a trace of self-pity in her voice, no bitterness for her hand-to-mouth childhood.

"I imagine this one will measure up."

"This is your first?" she asked, as she made her way to the half-finished cycle. She moved carefully, he noticed, her right leg dragging slightly, an indication of how tired she still must be even after her nap.

"Yep." He picked up a shop rag and squatted down to clean up an oil spill from the concrete floor. He didn't want her or Matty to take a tumble here, or anyplace else. "Last year I was in the hospital having the pins taken out of my ankle and before that, I was in Iraq. I got some of the artillery guys in the unit to e-mail Gus pointers on range and elevation, though, and they got a kick out of the pictures Joann sent back. Evidently a well-built trebuchet can get a lot of splat out of a past-its-prime jack-o'-lantern." He stood up and grabbed a handful of wrenches and screwdrivers he'd left lying on the tool bench.

"Would you prefer Matty and I not come down here for the party?" she asked quietly.

He dropped the tools in a drawer and shut it before turning around. Sarah had her back to him, looking down at the Indian, her fingers tracing the elegant curve of the chrome handlebars.

"Why would you think that?"

She darted a look at Matty, who was playing with a toy motorcycle Arlene had bought for him in the hospital gift shop the day after Sarah's surgery. He was running it up and down the seat of Joann's lumpy old futon, turning it into a motocross course, making engine noises and paying them no attention whatsoever.

"Your sisters aren't comfortable with me around, we both know it. Your mother, too, for that matter, although she's been trying her best to hide it. You'll have friends here, neighbors. People who will be wondering about our marriage. It's awkward for you, for your sisters. For all of us."

"So your solution is to hide out in the trailer?"

She lifted her head. "It wouldn't be hiding out. I just thought the less they see of me the easier I'll be forgotten when Matty and I leave."

"You've never been easy to forget, Sarah," he said quietly.

What little color the cold October air had brought to her cheeks faded away. He wished he'd kept his mouth shut but the words had seemed to leap past his tongue before he could stop them. She turned back to the motorcycle again. "You know what I mean, Nate."

He hooked his welding helmet onto a nail on the wall. "Come to the party, Sarah. I think I can handle the scrutiny." He wondered if he should tell her about Kaylene Jensen. She was a friend of Joann's from the bank. His friend, too, he supposed. They'd dated off and on, shared some good times, but it had never been serious, at least not on his part. He decided to keep the information to himself—after all, they hadn't seen each other since the middle of summer. It would probably just make Sarah more determined than ever to stay holed up in the trailer if she knew his old girlfriend was coming to the party.

"Mommy, let's go. I'm hungry." Matty had tired of the motorcycle and thrown it down on the futon. "Carry me," he pleaded, holding up his hands.

"I can't, sweetie. Not until my neck is better." Sarah took both his hands and pulled him close for a hug.

"I'm tired. I want you to carry me."

"I'll carry you," Nate offered.

"Want Mama," Matty said stubbornly.

"I'm feeling a lot stronger—" She didn't look stronger, the skin was pulled tight over her cheekbones and there were dark circles under her eyes. She had probably overdone it at rehab. Nate wished he'd been there to give the therapist a heads-up on her determination to make a record-breaking recovery, but she had insisted he drop her off at the clinic and pick her up when her session was finished, not hang around—acting like a husband.

"How about a piggyback ride? I give great piggyback rides."

"No," Matty insisted, but he looked as if he could be coaxed.

"I'll hold your hand the whole way," Sarah promised. "I bet Becca loves Nate's piggyback rides."

"Becca's a girl."

Nate dropped to his knees, ignoring the strain on ruined tendons and ligaments. "That's right, buddy. I think a real man like you would rather ride on my shoulders."

Nate was rewarded for his discomfort with a beaming smile. "Yeah, on your shoulders," Matty said.

Nate held out his hand and the little boy placed his much smaller one trustingly on his palm. He swung Matty up onto his shoulders, hearing him squeal with excitement and delicious fear as he stood up. Matty's head almost touched the ceiling. He curled his fingers in Nate's hair and held on for dear life.

"Ouch," Nate yelped, surprised at the strength of Matty's grip.

"Not so tight," Sarah said, laughing as she pried his fingers loose. "You'll pull Nate's hair out and then he'll be as bald as Grandpa Harm."

"Okay," Matty said, relaxing a little, "but don't drop me."

"I won't, buddy. Let's go."

Sarah held the door open and turned out the lights behind them, then slid the dead bolt home and handed him the key. "Look at the pretty sunset, Matty. See all the colors—orange and pink and in-digo." It was a beautiful sunset, the colors soft and muted as the short October twilight faded into night.

"What's *indigo?*" Matty demanded.

"Dark blue. The strip of clouds there at the bottom. The one that's almost the same color as the lake."

"Blue. I know blue. Let's go home," Matty said, losing interest in the view.

"Yes, let's go home." Sarah repeated in her soft musical voice, and the words sent a surge of longing through Nate that surprised him with its intensity.

Home, with Sarah and Matty. That's what he wanted. To be able to provide a place to keep them safe and warm, to laugh with them, to love them. His home. His wife. His child. *At least for a little while.*

CHAPTER FIVE

"INCOMING!"

"My Lord, haven't they run out of pumpkins yet?" Arlene asked, sliding onto the seat of the picnic table that a couple of Harm's renters had dragged up the hill earlier in the day, as yet another shriveled jack-o'-lantern sailed heavenward to land with a resounding splat thirty feet down the slope.

It was the kind of autumn afternoon Texas-born Sarah had read about but never experienced. The air was clear and bracing, cold enough for her to be thankful for the winter coat Arlene had loaned her until she could go shopping for one of her own. The ground beneath their feet was thick with red and gold leaves, and off in the distance the sound of a chainsaw competed with the whoops and shouts of the dozen or so teenagers gathered around their scale-model siege weapon at the bottom of the hill.

Her mother-in-law set a disposable cup in front of her. "I brought you some cider. Be careful, it's hot."

Sarah moved her camera out of the way and

smiled her thanks. The cider was the color of autumn sunshine and redolent of cinnamon and cloves. She took a careful sip. "Umm, that's wonderful."

"I know. Our next-door neighbor's in-laws have a press on their farm. Jack and Carmen Wilhelm. They're standing over there under the oak tree. He's wearing the leather duster and cowboy hat. Have you met them yet?"

"I believe I did…before," Sarah said, disgusted with herself for hesitating over the answer.

"Oh, yes. Certainly you did. They were invited to the reception we gave for you and Nate the first time you were married." Arlene paused, then plowed on. "We get a couple of gallons fresh pressed every year."

"I've never seen a cider press," Sarah admitted. It was awkward, this before-and-after talk, but there didn't seem to be any easy way to get around it.

Arlene was trying, too. Her voice was determinedly cheerful when she replied. "I should have asked you and Matty to ride along with Tom and me when we went to get it. He would have enjoyed a trip to the farm. They have goats and chickens and a couple of horses. I'm sorry I didn't think of it. I'll probably stop out there again before Thanksgiving. I'll be sure and let you know when I do."

"We'd like that," Sarah said, and she meant it. She wanted to keep on good terms with Nate's family. She was thinking more and more of staying in the area when she and Matty were on their own again. There was no particular reason to go back to Texas, and no HomeContractor franchises where David's sister lived, so she didn't see that as an option.

"That last one was great! Did you hear it Grandma? It sounded like a big whistling meteor, or alien spaceship, or something," Ty announced as he and his brother came running up. They'd been playing on the deck of the trailer along with Matty and Becca, who were being watched over by Nate's teenage cousin, Erika. A half dozen other children scampered up and down the hill between pumpkin barrages, or wandered in and out of the open double doors of the barn.

"Or something," Arlene agreed. "At least they aren't blaring that horrible music this year."

"What music is that?" Sarah didn't think Arlene was referring to "Hail to the Victors," the Michigan fight song, which was coming through the speakers of a CD player set up near the barn doors.

"Why The Smashing Pumpkins naturally. One of the great alternative bands of all time, in my humble opinion." Tessa's husband, Keith, leaned both hands on the table. He was tall and lanky, balding a little on top. "The music of my youth, but Mother Fowler put the kibosh on any more heavy metal music."

"I did not. I only said there had to be something better to listen to. And don't call me Mother Fowler. It makes me feel older than dirt."

"Roger that, Mom," he said with a grin, completely unfazed by Arlene's indignation. He pointed to Sarah's camera. "Getting any good pictures?"

"I think I am. Kids are always great subjects, and the background couldn't be better. The trees are gorgeous." All the shades of an autumn rainbow ringed the lakeshore—green and yellow, gold and brown and the scarlet-purple of maple and sumac. Out on the lake a lone pontoon skimmed along the water heading for the yacht club, on one last excursion before being put away for the season. All along the shoreline she could see docks piled like so much cordwood, and boats hauled up alongside them covered with blue and green and silver plastic tarps to protect them from winter's snow and ice.

"I'll be glad to pay you for the prints if the ones you took of Becca and Tessa by the rock wall turn out as good as I think they will."

"No way," she said, with a wave of her hand. "I owe you and Tessa so much for helping to look after Matty. They'll be my gift."

"Okay. It's a deal."

"Keith, we need some input down here." Nate's voice seemed to come out of thin air.

His brother-in-law held up a walkie-talkie. "I'm

the spotter in case you hadn't guessed. Time to get back to work." He toggled the switch. "Nate, tell Gus he needs another degree of elevation. Next one should stay right on target then."

"One degree up," Nate's voice repeated. "Clear the firing range."

"Will do." Keith headed off, signaling Harm and the elderly couple he was with to wait for the next shot.

"Honestly, he's as bad as the children," Arlene said, shaking her head at Keith's back as he walked away, but she was smiling indulgently. "I'd love to have some of the pictures of Matty and my grandchildren, too. The ones you took of them in their Halloween costumes were adorable."

The pictures had been good. At the last moment she'd decided not to pass out candy at the trailer, but instead had gone to Arlene and Tom's and watched from the porch as Nate walked Matty up and down the block. The shot that she liked the best, the one that was most special to her, was of Matty in his furry green ogre suit, wide-eyed and smiling with excitement as he tugged Nate forward, eager to show her his bag of treats. Nate had been smiling, too, and it was what she saw in his eyes as he gazed at her son that made the picture so precious to her. It was love. She knew in her heart it was.

Sarah brought her rosy musings to an abrupt halt. The fact that Nate was beginning to care for her son, just as she had prayed he would during the dark days of her illness, didn't change the untenable situation between the two of them, and she would do well to remember that.

"I'll bring these over when I get them developed and you can choose the ones you'd like to have prints of."

"Wonderful."

"Bull's-eye!" Jack hollered, jumping up and down as the next orange missile scored a direct hit. "That one was really gross. Did you see, Grammie? It was all black inside and the face was caved in. Awesome."

Arlene shuddered. "I saw it. Ugh."

"The blue team's getting really good at homing in on the target. That's 'cause Uncle Nate's army buddies showed my dad how to get the trebuchet really smoking. They say a trebuchet was a weapon of mass destruction back in Robin Hood's day." Ty squinted one eye shut and sighted along his outstretched arm. "Bam. Bam. Bam. I can't wait until I'm old enough to be in Dad's science club so I can be the one to yank the firing cord. It will be awesome."

"Then you'll have to get better grades on your math papers. Remember your dad told you there's lots of figuring involved in getting that thing aimed right," Arlene reminded him.

"I know," Ty looked crestfallen for a moment, then brightened. "I'll do better this week, you'll see."

"I know you will." Arlene snaked her arm around his waist for a quick hard hug before he pulled away.

"Jeez, Gram, I'm too old for that."

"Not for me, you aren't."

"Get ready. Here they go again," Jack yelled.

Sarah and Arlene turned their attention to the activity around the trebuchet. It really was an impressive piece of equipment. Made of two-by-fours with wooden wheels on both sides, it was larger than Sarah had expected, standing almost six feet high. The weighted throwing arm and canvas sling were nearly double that. It had arrived in the back of Gus's pickup truck with a retinue of a dozen junior and senior members of the science club.

A few hours earlier, as she cut up chunks of cheese and arranged olives and pickles for a relish tray, Sarah had watched from the kitchen window while the guests stopped at the bottom of the hill where the trebuchet was set up next to Harm's fire pit. They dropped off their pumpkins, some now painted in scarlet and gray to represent the despised Ohio State Buckeyes, before proceeding on to the barn to unload casserole dishes and coolers, and take up positions in folding chairs and at picnic tables to watch the show.

Then it had been her turn to be the center of attention as she carried the plastic-covered tray from the trailer to the barn, running the gauntlet of stares and greetings from Nate's friends and neighbors, some friendly, come curious. She'd made the nerve-racking journey without a misstep or a stumble, the result of long hours of therapy on her weakened leg, but the experience had left her sweaty-palmed and trembling. If it hadn't been for Nate standing stead-fastly in the shadow of the big double doors she might have turned tail and limped back to the trailer.

When he'd come toward her to take the tray, she'd braced herself for him to scold her for not waiting for his help. Instead he leaned forward and said in a voice meant for her ears alone, "I would have come to help you but I knew you'd roast my butt in front of everyone if I did."

She'd opened her mouth to fling back a retort but then he smiled and she forgot what she was going to say, almost forgot to breathe. It was the same devas-tating smile, starting with just a curve of his lips and then spreading to encompass his whole mouth, that had always set her heart aflutter and, heaven help her, still did.

Electricity ran along her skin at the recollection. It seemed the stronger she got, the more often she thought about Nate in a sexual way. The sound of his voice, the brush of his hand on her arm. Day or night. Waking or sleeping. She couldn't seem to help herself.

"Sarah, watch out!" Arlene called. Reality jumped back into focus. Sarah lifted her arms to shield her face as an off-target pumpkin disintegrated into dozens of globs of orange pulp almost at their feet.

"Awesome," Ty yelled, raising his fists high above his head and doing a victory dance. "That one almost got us."

"Cripes, this is liable to give me flashbacks to Korea, what with all the yelling, and ducking and running for cover. I'm getting too old for this, and that damned catapult or whatever ya call it is digging holes in my yard," Harm grumbled as he settled himself heavily beside his daughter.

"Dad's pulling your leg, Sarah. He loves parties. And in case you missed it, Gus always lets him shoot off the first pumpkin."

"Dead on bull's-eye. Haven't lost my touch." The old man winked at Sarah. "It's going to take all day tomorrow to clean up the mess. Glad it's Gus and his kids and not me doing the shoveling. What ya drinking?" he asked, leaning over to peer into Arlene's cup.

"Cider. Do you want some?"

"Nah, gives me gas. I think I'll have me a beer pretty soon. Wonder how many more of them things they're going to fling on up here? Poor old Buster'll be afraid to come home for a week."

"Dad's cat lost one of his nine lives the first year

Gus did this. A pumpkin split in two on take-off and half of it came down within six inches of Buster's nose. He's never forgotten," Arlene explained.

Harm squinted into the hazy glare of the sun hanging just above the horizon on the far side of the lake. "I'm getting hungry."

"Then I'm just in time." Nate's father walked up to the table. His face was red and he smelled of smoke from tending the huge cast-iron kettle of beef stew hanging from a tripod over the fire blazing in a corner of the parking lot. "The hobo stew's just about done, and they're starting to set the food out on the tables," he informed his wife. He nodded toward the fire where Nate's Uncle Dan and a man Sarah had never met were swinging the container off the flame and carrying it into the barn.

"I should get my seven-layer salad mixed up then." Arlene rose and, taking her husband's out-stretched hand, hurried away, leaving Sarah alone with Harm.

"Getting chilly sitting out here now that the sun's going down," he remarked, turning up the collar of his red-and-black plaid wool coat that looked to Sarah not to be many years younger than the man who wore it. "Want to come inside with me and scout out the dessert table?"

"I should check on Matty first. He's probably get-ting hungry, too."

"I'm getting stiff sitting here. I'll walk over to the trailer with you and work out the kinks."

"I'd like that." She had seen more of Harm than the rest of Nate's family the last couple of weeks and she felt comfortable in his company. He always waved and called a greeting, sometimes even walked up the hill to chat a few moments if she was outside playing with Matty.

Before they could leave the picnic table, Erika, pretty and blond and sporting three earrings in her left ear, came walking up with Becca and Matty each hanging onto her hands. "Hi, Grandpa."

"Hi, girlie. She's the spitting image of her grandmother, Lord rest her soul," he told Sarah. "You in charge of these two?" he asked, pointing to the little ones.

Becca was wearing a parka the color of ripe grapes and a fuzzy purple hat and mittens. Matty had on a miniature Detroit Lions jacket and his now indispensable ball cap. Joann had brought a box of her sons' outgrown clothes to the trailer a few days before, offering them in an offhand manner as though she expected Sarah to refuse. When Sarah had asked her to come inside she'd done so reluctantly, but seemed relieved when Sarah told her how grateful she was for the gift. When she confided to Joann that outfitting Matty for the long, cold winter ahead had been one of her chief concerns, Nate's sister had agreed to stay long enough to have a cup of coffee, and help sort through the garments she thought would fit Matty now, and those that could be put away for next summer.

She had even confided to Sarah the reason she was cleaning out her drawers and closets was because she might be pregnant again and would need the storage space for the new baby's things. Sarah had promised not to tell a soul about the pregnancy, an easy one to keep since she rarely spoke to anyone but Nate and her therapist.

It had been a good first step in reestablishing a relationship with Joann, especially since the other woman had made the initial effort. Sarah didn't fool herself into thinking that all was forgiven and forgotten between them, but it was a start. It wasn't until later, when she was putting the freshly washed clothes into Matty's drawers, that she realized how much she envied Joann and Tessa their pregnancies. She had enjoyed being pregnant, remembered the wonder of holding Matty in her arms for the first time, feeling him tug hungrily at her breast as she nursed him. She would like to experience that joy again.

She had sat there on the side of the bed staring out the window at the ravine behind the trailer, seeing nothing, thinking only that miracles came in all sizes and shapes. Only three weeks before, she had been prepared to die, and now she was dreaming of some-day having another child.

"Can I take Matty down to the creek to see the dam pool?" Erika was asking her. "I'll be careful with him. Jack and Ty are already down there throwing rocks in the water."

The creek ran between narrow banks behind the trailer. "Is it safe for you to play down there?" Sarah asked.

"There's steps and a railing. Nate built them so they're secure."

"The kids like to play down there. It's okay," Harm assured her. "Good skating in the winter."

"Tessa already said it was fine for me to take Becca."

"Then I guess it will be all right, but please don't let go of his hand."

"Don't worry, I'll take good care of him."

"We'll be along in a few minutes to call you back to eat," Harm informed his granddaughter. "It looks as if they're done flinging pumpkins into the wild blue yonder for another year."

Sarah glanced over her shoulder. Nate, Gus and Keith were helping the science club members to load the trebuchet back onto the truck. Then the truck followed by a second one full of teenagers, pulled slowly out onto the road, returning the siege engine to its storage unit at the high school, while the rest of the school kids grabbed plastic garbage bags and began cleaning up the remains of the pumpkins.

"Halloween is officially over." Both Harm and Sarah turned their heads to look at the petite redhead, about Sarah's own age, who had seated herself at their table. She held out her hand. "Hi, I'm Kaylene Jensen, Joann's friend—and Nate's," she said. "You must be Sarah."

"Yes, I am." Sarah shook the proffered hand.

"I wanted to offer you my congratulations on your recovery." She smiled and it almost reached her deep green eyes, but not quite. "And on your marriage."

"Thank you." Who was this woman? Sarah wondered. Introducing herself as Nate's friend could mean so many things. She wished he was here to give her a cue as how to proceed.

"I guess if I'm going to be accurate I should be congratulating you on your remarriage."

"I don't remember meeting you when Nate and I were married before," Sarah said, refusing to rise to the bait. "Have you been friends a long time?" What she really wanted to ask was had she been his lover. The thought startled her, and what shocked her even more was the emotion behind it. It was jealousy, pure and simple, and she had no excuse for feeling it.

"I've only lived in the area for the last two years. Nate and I dated for awhile. He told me a little bit about you." Sarah was surprised by that and it must have shown. "I mean he told me that he had been married but it hadn't worked out. He never said anything about you two getting back together." Kaylene's voice remained polite and friendly, but Sarah saw the flash of confusion and pain in her eyes that she wasn't quite able to hide. And suddenly she felt more sorrow than anger for the woman. It was evident, at least to Sarah, that Kaylene cared for Nate, possibly even loved him, or thought she did, and she was more upset than she wanted to appear.

"That's because we lost touch until very recently."

"Love at first sight all over again?" Hurt won out over pride and the edges of Kaylene's words were sharp as broken glass.

Nate had told her there was no woman in his life when he had agreed to marry her again and she had believed him, because she needed to, and wanted to so desperately. But had she been wrong? Had he sacrificed a relationship for her sake and Matty's? Had she come between him and a woman he might have fallen in love with one day soon?

Harm rose heavily to his feet. "C'mon, Sarah, time for us to go round up them grandkids of mine. If one of them slips and falls in the crick there'll be hell to pay."

She grabbed at Harm's lifeline before she said something that betrayed how tenuous her place in

Nate's life actually was. "It was nice meeting you, Kaylene."

"I'm sure we'll see more of each other. The Fowlers have the best parties in Riley's Cove this time of year. I never miss any of them." Kaylene smiled again, and as before it wasn't reflected in her eyes. She waited for Sarah to stand up before rising gracefully herself. She laid her hand on the sleeve of Harm's old coat. "I brought the pumpkin cheesecake you liked so well last year. Save room for a piece."

"Sure thing. See you later, Kaylene." He pointed toward a break in the tree line at the far corner of Nate's property and motioned Sarah to follow him as the other woman turned on her heel and headed back toward the barn. "That's where the kids are." He walked slowly across the rough ground, urging Sarah to watch her step. "Used to be a chicken coop and machine shed up here. Fell down years ago. Nate had them bulldozed when he bought the property from old Frank Heller."

"Is that the man who got him interested in restoring old motorcycles?"

"Yeah. Nate was at loose ends when he got out of the hospital. Couldn't get around all that good on his bum leg. He's always been a first-rate mechanic. Worked for Frank when he was a kid in high school. Frank had a good business putting classic bikes back together for collectors all over the eastern half of the country. A lot of contacts, that's what you need in a business like that. But his wife was dying of cancer and he wanted to spend his time with her so he turned the business over to Nate. He's done good with it this last year. The one he's working on now is the biggest commission he's gotten so far. The money will go a long way toward getting started on the renovations to the barn."

"He's going to expand his workshop?"

Harm stopped walking and turned his head to look at her from faded brown eyes. His expression was quizzical. "He wants to live there, Sarah. Hasn't he shown you the plans for turning it into his home? You didn't think he was going to be living in a trailer the rest of his life, did you?"

"No." Sarah felt a weight settle into her chest, just about where she thought her heart must be. Nate hadn't told her about his scheme for turning the old barn into a home. He hadn't told her the details of how he came to own his own business, or how successful it had become.

He hadn't told her about Kaylene Jensen and that bothered her most of all.

Harm stayed where he was as the long twilight shadows reached out toward them from the creek bank, an old man who had seen a lot in his lifetime and who could probably read the thoughts racing across her mind. The sounds of music and laughing voices spilled out of the barn. The smells of wood smoke and rich stew eddied around them in the cold air. Ahead, Sarah could hear Jack and Ty shouting and the splash of rocks being thrown into the water, but where they stood, she and Nate's grandfather were cocooned in silence.

"What are you planning to do when you're back on your feet, Sarah? Have you and Nate talked about your future at all?" Harm asked in a gruff but gentle voice.

Now Sarah could hear Matty's laughter mingling with the others, higher pitched, more excited. She wanted to hurry to him, make sure Erika was being as vigilant as she'd promised about keeping him away from the dark, cold water of the creek, but her feet remained firmly rooted to the spot. The weight in her chest grew a little heavier, like a stone.

What would she do with her life once she was on her own again? She hadn't dared to think that far ahead, because it seemed like a long stretch of years to spend on her own, but she had to tell Harm the truth. She owed that to Nate's grandfather. He loved his grandson and didn't want to see him hurt again. "We haven't talked about the future because we don't have one."

CHAPTER SIX

NATE LEANED one shoulder against a beam and looked around him. Only a half-dozen or so people remained in the barn, all of them busy taking down tables and stacking folding chairs against the wall, ready to be loaded into pickups and returned to the Riley's Cove Volunteer Fire Department in the morning. Keith was singing along to an Alan Jackson album on the CD player, bagging up trash and sorting empty returnable pop cans out of the debris, while Harm was making sure the last of the coals from the bonfire were out before heading back to his place.

Someone had dragged the old futon out of his workshop for extra seating and Erika was curled up in one corner with a sleeping Matty in her lap. Arlene had taken Tessa and Becca home an hour ago but Jack and Ty were still on their feet. They'd run out of steam, though, and Joann was herding them both out to the truck. They looked like a couple of miniature zombies, dull-eyed and stiff-legged, Nate thought with a grin.

Sarah was nowhere to be seen.

"Gus and the kids will be back tomorrow to scrape up the last of the pumpkin crap," Joann said. She looked tired but happy. She hadn't made an announcement of her pregnancy, but had confided to him earlier that the second, and definitive test, had been positive.

"Don't worry about the mess." He reached out and pulled Ty against his leg, wrapping his arm around his shoulder. "Your mom and Aunt Tessa put on great parties don't they, partner?"

"Yep," Ty mumbled sleepily. "It was a blast." He rested his head against Nate's side. His nephew was growing up fast, Nate realized with a little shock how quickly time was passing. He was going to be tall, like the Fowler side of the family.

"It did go well. Thanks for letting us use the barn."

"My pleasure."

His sister looked up at the oak-beamed ceiling and the hayloft that he hoped someday would be his master suite with a view out over the rolling countryside of the Irish Hills. "I never would have envisioned living here. Now I wish I'd thought of it first. It'll be a great house when you get it done, Nate. Sarah thinks so, too, you know. She's got a couple of good ideas for improving on your floor plan. You should talk to her about them."

"I didn't even know Sarah had seen the drawings." He hadn't shown them to her. He couldn't even remember the subject coming up. Most of their conversations were general in nature, small talk, really. Nothing personal. It was as if they existed in a sort of limbo these days, marking time. Sarah seemed to be waiting for her final visit to the surgeon before making her move to be on her own again. He didn't know what he was waiting for. Some kind of divine inspiration on why she and Matty should stay with him? So far it hadn't happened. Outside of telling her the truth—that he was pretty sure he was starting to fall in love with her all over again—he'd drawn a complete blank.

"We were looking at the drawings this evening. I guess you could say Kaylene sweet-talked me into getting them out." Joann frowned a little and he realized he was, too. "Was that okay?"

He made himself smile. "Not a problem."

"Did I hear someone take my name in vain?" Kaylene had come up behind them as they talked.

"Joann was just telling me you were looking over the plans for the renovations."

"We were. I hope you don't mind." She looked up at him, her expression half-apology, half-challenge.

"I don't mind. I like the input."

"Good, I want us to stay friends." She put her hand on his arm. She was smaller than Sarah, petite and fine-boned, a year or two older, he guessed, although he had never asked, and Kaylene had never told him her age. "There've been so many people around tonight I haven't been able to congratulate you on your marriage until now. Congratulations, Nate." She raised up on tiptoe and gave him a kiss full on the lips.

Joann's mouth opened and shut. Then she made a shooing motion with both hands, urging the boys toward the truck. "I'd better be going." When Ty didn't budge she took him by the hand, tugging him away from Nate's side.

"I'll walk with you, Jo." It was the coward's way out and he knew it.

"No need." Gus moved from the shadows near the doors into the circle of light where they were standing. His brother-in-law was six inches shorter and twenty-five pounds lighter than Nate but he swung Jack up into his arms with little effort. "It's way past bedtime for these guys and they've got Sunday school tomorrow. I'll be back after church with my press gang to finish cleaning up. We appreciate you putting up with us."

"I already told Joann I was happy to do it."

With a final chorus of "good-nights" Joann and her family disappeared into the darkness beneath the old oak tree.

"You're parked down by the lake, aren't you?" Nate said. "I'll walk you to your car." He owed Kaylene an explanation and he should have given it long before this.

"My cooler's back there." She pointed to the place where the food tables had been set up.

"I'll drop it off tomorrow when we take the table and chairs back to the firehouse."

"All right." She shifted her small purse to her right shoulder and slipped her other arm through his. "I'm ready then."

The moonlight was faint, pale and silvery, as cold as the frost that sparkled on every surface. They walked in silence for a while, each watching their step until their eyes adjusted to the darkness. "I wish you had told me about Sarah," Kaylene said at last. "I didn't deserve to hear about your marriage over the water cooler at the bank." She gave a brittle little laugh. "And it wasn't even Joann who told me."

"It all happened very quickly, Kaylene, but that's no excuse. I owed you a call. I'm sorry."

"A call?" She stopped beside her car, a sporty little red Mazda he'd helped her pick out in the spring, and swung around to face him. "Is that all I meant to you? That you owed me a phone call to tell me you'd married another woman on what seemed to be about thirty minutes notice? The same woman I would have bet my last dollar had broken your heart?"

"Sarah's condition was grave. I had no choice."

She rubbed her finger along the top of the car door making a dark streak in the frost crystals. "Are you planning to stay married to her?"

"We don't know what we're going to do about the marriage, Kaylene." That was the hell of it. What lay in store for them? More heartache? The chance for a new beginning? Or two lives going in separate directions?

"Was I wrong thinking we were on our way to being more than just friends?" Her voice had lost most of its edge. Her expression was proud but the corners of her mouth trembled.

His gut churned with shame and remorse. She was fun to be around, smart, savvy, a good sport. He had enjoyed her company, and he had enjoyed the sex. So had she. But he also knew she wanted marriage, a family, children. In his mind's eye he saw again the longing in her eyes when she came across the antique rocking horse at the yacht club flea market during the Fourth of July celebration that summer. He knew he could never give her all those things she wanted, and so he had begun to pull away. That was long before Sarah had come back into his life, but he couldn't tell Kaylene that, either, without hurting her more than he already had.

"We didn't really have a chance, did we?" she said, answering her own question. "I thought we did, but something changed this summer. Something made you start to back off? I never could figure out what it was. Maybe now I know. Was it because of her? Because of Sarah?"

He didn't contradict her because there was a lot of truth in what she said. He had never gotten over Sarah, never would. "It doesn't do us any good to talk about what might have been. It's too late. I'm married to Sarah. It's a fact that can't be changed."

"Not if you don't want it to be."

"I don't know what I want," Nate said truthfully.

"I know what you don't want." She threw back her shoulders, pulling her car keys out of the pocket of her suede jacket. She beeped open the lock. "I should apologize for the kiss back there. I was out of line."

"You don't have to apologize to me."

"I didn't mean you." She giggled. Too late he caught the sparkle of mischief in her green eyes. "I meant I should apologize to your wife."

"I'll explain to her."

"I hope so. I'm not nearly as silver-tongued as I'd like to think I am, and I got the impression she'll fight for what she wants." She reached up and laid her hand against his cheek. She was wearing gloves and the leather was soft and supple against his skin. "You don't have to worry I'll cause trouble between you and Sarah, Nate. It's not my style."

"It would have surprised the hell out of me if you did."

"I'd like us to stay friends. Cottonwood Lake is too small to avoid each other, anyway."

"I'd like that, too, Kaylene." Nate put his hands on her shoulders and kissed her very softly on the cheek.

She clung to him for a moment. "I meant it when I wished you the best." She moved back a step and he opened the car door. "Goodbye," she said. "And good luck. I think you're going to need it." The engine turned over and a moment later she was gone.

"ARE YOU HERE ALL ALONE?" Nate was standing in the doorway of his workshop. Sarah looked over her shoulder at him. She was sitting on the futon with her legs pulled up under her to ward off the chill. Matty was curled up by her side, still wearing his beloved Michigan hat, his thumb in his mouth.

"I didn't hear you come in," she said. He hadn't been gone very long, really, but it had seemed like ages when she had nothing else to do but speculate on what he was saying to the red-haired woman that she was now convinced was more than half in love with him. The question remained: Was Nate in love with her?

"I came through the side door. I wanted to lock up the workshop. Is everyone else gone?" He looked around, his words echoing slightly in the big empty space.

"Your dad left about ten minutes ago. Your Uncle Dan took Erika home right after that. Matty and I were just waiting for you to come back for us, weren't we?"

"Carry me," Matty mumbled, still half-asleep.

"I'll carry you, buddy." Nate held out his arms and Matty reached up to him without hesitation. Nate scooped him up against his chest and Matty wrapped his arms around his neck, laying his head on Nate's shoulder, asleep again between one heartbeat and the next. Sarah felt her heart swell as she watched her son being cradled in Nate's strong embrace. He looked so right there. She closed her eyes and tried to imagine David in his place. The image wouldn't form. Sadness overcame her momentarily. *I'm sorry, David.* She would be grateful always that he had given her a son but they had shared so little time together and it was harder with each day that passed to keep his memory from fading from her thoughts.

"Sarah, do you need some help?" Nate was holding out his hand.

She blinked away the emotion and put her hand in his. She stood up and made a face as she put her weight on her right leg. "Ouch."

"Anything wrong?" There was immediate concern in Nate's low, deep tone.

She looked at him and smiled. "My foot's asleep. I hate when that happens, don't you?"

"Do you need a minute?" Nate was watching her closely, as he always did, gauging her mood, her level of fatigue.

It had been a long, busy day. But she was only tired, nothing more, nothing a good night's sleep wouldn't mend. She swung her camera strap onto her shoulder and gave her head a little shake. "I'm fine. A little stiff and chilly, that's all."

Tom had closed the big double doors after he and Gus moved the futon back into the workshop, so that task was taken care of. Nate shut off the lights and locked the smaller door while Sarah waited with her hands in her pockets. She needed to buy gloves, too, before winter really set in. "All buttoned up for the night." Nate put his hand on the small of her back and she felt the warmth of it through the layers of clothes she wore. Or at least she imagined she did.

"I enjoyed myself today," she said as they stood in the shadow of the barn letting their eyes adjust to the moon-dappled darkness of the yard.

"You didn't expect to, did you?" Nate asked, as they began walking slowly toward the trailer. She resisted the urge to twine her arm through his as Kaylene had done. Instead she held herself straight and tall, walking without a limp or a misstep across the uneven ground that had often tripped her up not so many days before. A train whistle sounded far off in the distance and there were car lights moving along the shore road, but here on the top of the hill it was so quiet she could hear their footsteps, crunching slightly on the frosty grass.

She looked up at him. He knew her too well. "I wanted to crawl into bed and pull the covers over my head if you must know the truth. I didn't want to answer a lot of questions about my illness, about our marriage. Now that everything's turned out so well it all seems so melodramatic somehow. Like a made-for-TV movie, or a tabloid story."

"Hey," he said feigning indignation. "This is my life you're talking about."

"I'm sorry, I was just trying to explain how I felt."

"Yeah, I know. Stuff like this doesn't happen very often around here. You have to expect people are going to be interested to see how it all turns out."

She wanted to ask him how he thought it was going to turn out but didn't have the courage. "I'm glad I didn't stayed holed up in the trailer. I was wrong about your friends and neighbors—they were all great, friendly and helpful. Your family was nice, too, Nate. I appreciated how hard they tried to include me in everything."

"They're happy for you, Sarah. Glad your recovery is going so well."

But would they be happier when she walked out of Nate's life again? For the first time today she had let herself hope, just a little, that they might not be.

That she could mend her fragile relationship with Nate's family, gain a place within their loving, protective circle for her son. She voiced the wish aloud. "I would like to think we could all be friends again, when we dissolve this marriage."

Nate stiffened a little and Matty stirred against his shoulder. "It's all right, buddy. Go back to sleep. It's pretty hard for a man and woman to stay just friends with a history like ours."

She slowed her steps, saw him moving away from her into the darkness, shutting her out—or sealing himself in? "Nate." He stopped at the bottom of the steps leading up to the deck and turned toward her. "Why didn't you tell me about your plans for the barn?"

He shrugged. "We had more important things to deal with."

"Not lately, not for the past ten days."

"Are you angry that Kaylene Jensen was the one who told you about them?" he asked, catching her off guard in his turn.

"I'm not angry." She could be as evasive as he was. She walked past him up the steps.

"Liar," he said quietly, as she opened the door to the warmth and light of the trailer's small living room. He waited for her reaction, watching her from fathomless gray eyes.

"You're wrong. I wasn't angry, but I was embarrassed." She took off Arlene's old coat and hung it on a hook in the closet. She set her camera on the kitchen divider while he laid her sleeping child gently in the seat of his oversized chair, then turned to face her.

"I'm sorry," he said. "I made a mess of that whole situation. I should have had the decency to tell Kaylene about our marriage as soon as I knew you were going to be okay. I didn't."

"Did Matty and I coming into your life spoil it for the two of you, Nate? Can you still make it right with her?" She hated saying those words, but her conscience wouldn't let them remain unspoken.

"There wasn't anything to spoil, Sarah." He shrugged out of his canvas jacket and hung it beside hers in the closet.

"I'm not so sure about that. I saw her kiss you, Nate. It was more than just friendly." *It was the way she dreamed of kissing him again.* She knelt in front of the chair to take off Matty's shoes and hat. She leaned forward so that her hair brushed her cheeks and hid the rush of color she couldn't control. She had been doing so well, staying calm and reasoned, but just like in the old days her emotions had betrayed her.

"That's right. You saw *her* kiss *me*. As a matter of fact she offered to apologize to you for it."

"She did?" That surprised her. She rocked back on her heels and looked up at him.

He wasn't quite smiling, but some of the darkness

was gone from his gray eyes. "She didn't want you to get the wrong impression. She was just saying goodbye."

"And you're willing to let her go. Just like that?"

"Whatever there was between us was over months ago. But I wasn't man enough to make the break clean and neat. I don't like admitting it, but that's how it was."

He hated being in the wrong, he hadn't changed in that respect, but in the old days he would have turned on his heel and walked away from the discussion, yet tonight he was doing his best to explain.

"Then you wouldn't have married her one day? You aren't in love with her?"

"No," he said, reaching down to pull her to her feet. "I'm not in love with her. I wouldn't have fallen in love with her next week, next month, or next year. Your coming here to Cottonwood Lake didn't doom the second great love affair of my life."

She had been the great love of his life. Her heart raced in her chest and she felt as light-headed and dizzy as she had the first few days after her surgery. "I wish you had told me about your dreams for the barn, Nate," she said quietly as his eyes held hers and his arms rested warmly on her shoulders.

"There's still time for telling each other about our dreams, Sarah. Maybe that's one of the things we can do better this time around."

Panic fluttered along her nerve endings. She couldn't listen to her heart, she must heed her mind. "Nate, we can't go back and change the past."

"All right. We can't go back. But we can go forward."

"I'm not stay—"

"I know. You're not staying. Why not?" His mouth came down on hers, soft and warm. She held herself still, didn't kiss him back. She was afraid to, afraid that once she tasted his lips, his mouth again, she would be lost, that all the plans for a life for her and Matty that she'd made so painstakingly these last weeks would drift out of her mind like smoke across the lake.

His kiss was gentle, testing, she could feel herself weakening, longing for so much more. She put her hands on his chest and broke the contact of their mouths. "I can't stay," she repeated stubbornly.

"Why?"

"Because you didn't tell me about your dream," she said helplessly. She knew she sounded as if she was spouting nonsense but she couldn't seem to gather her scattered thoughts into coherent sentences.

"I will," he said, his voice husky and dark in her ears, promising more than mere words, much more. "I'll tell you everything you want to know."

"And what do you want from me in return, Nate?"

"I want you to tell me yours."

CHAPTER SEVEN

THE LIGHT coming through the small jalousied window of his bedroom was liquid and gray, only a few shades lighter than the slice of sky he could see through the part in the curtains. Nate stretched his arms over his head and promptly banged his knuckles on the wall. He'd forgotten, again, that he was in the tiny second bedroom of the trailer, although when he turned his head the view overhead of the top bunk should have reminded him.

It hadn't, for the simple reason he was too focused on the sounds coming from beyond the thin wall, splashes and giggles and the low, sweet sound of Sarah's laughter. Matty was taking a bath. He folded his arms behind his head, letting himself fantasize for a minute or two that Matty was his son. He wondered how different his life might have been if he'd agreed to let Sarah try to become pregnant before he left for the Middle East? Would they still be together? It was a question he'd avoided for four long years, but now it kept constantly breaking into his thoughts.

He dropped his feet to the floor and pulled himself to a sitting position. It was a Norman Rockwell kind of fantasy and nothing but wishful thinking. If they had stayed together she wouldn't have Matty, or any child for that matter. That was what was so damned ironic about their breakup, the truth he'd learned after the accident. That he could never give her a child. Then or now.

He rubbed his hand across the stubble on his chin. All the heartache and misery they'd endured was for nothing. He was sterile, probably always had been and never knew it. Still wouldn't, if follow-up tests after a nasty post-op infection hadn't shown antibodies in his blood that shouldn't be there. There had been consultations with urologists and more tests—of a kind he'd rather forget—and when you sorted through the alphabet soup of blood work-ups and polysyllabic medical terms the bottom line was that he was allergic to his own sperm. As the guys in his old unit would put it, with a wink and a smirk, he was shooting blanks.

He couldn't have gotten Sarah pregnant even if he'd wanted to.

The sad part was he figured they would have ended up divorced anyway. There were just too many strikes against them back then to have made the outcome any different. He had been convinced he was always right, and she had been too uncertain of herself to stand up to him. What he would never know was how big a factor his sterility would have been in the final outcome. And God help him, he was still afraid to put himself in a position to find out.

SARAH WAS SITTING on the toilet seat, barefooted and wearing a pair of faded sweats and an equally faded sweatshirt, watching Matty splash and wiggle around like a little pink fish in the tub. Ninety percent of her attention was focused on her son, but a small part of her mind kept listening for sounds of movement from beyond the bathroom wall. "Time to get out, sweetie. Nate will be awake soon. He'll want to use the bathroom."

"No!" Matty's reply was direct and to the point. "My turn. Shrek's still dirty." He held up a plastic figure, one of several floating around him. "Wash Shrek. Please," he added with a dimpled smile that lit up her heart, and the dreary November morning.

"Okay, two more minutes." She handed him the washcloth he'd flopped over the side of the tub. "Don't forget to wash behind Shrek's ears. And yours." She put her elbows on her knees and rested her chin in her hands, staring at the towel rack on the far wall.

The bathroom was one place where Nate had been defeated in his attempts at a monochrome color scheme. The fixtures were original, the shade of green that had been known as Avocado in the seventies, and would probably be called Margarita Slush, or Martini, or some such on a paint chip card today. They were in good shape as far as Sarah could tell so that's probably why he hadn't replaced them, or the truly hideous pendant lights above the sink. Instead he'd settled for painting the paneling and vanity a creamy ivory and stopped there. The floor was covered with worn stone-patterned vinyl with tracings of green. The towels and shower curtain were the same color as the walls, making the tub and toilet stand out…like olives in a martini glass.

She would probably have wallpapered over the paneling, something tailored and understated, to suit Nate's tastes. Since she couldn't hide it, she'd play up the avocado with matching towels, or perhaps as a nod to Nate's monomania, a silvery-gray if she could find just the right shade. While she was at it, spending his money in her head, a glass enclosure for the tub would be nice, instead of the utilitarian vinyl shower curtain he'd chosen. She'd replace the faucets with aged-brass vintage-style spigots, add matching hardware on the vanity, and banish the lights to Goodwill in favor of track lighting on the ceiling. She might even try the faux marble painting technique on the floor that she'd learned in one of her department's continuing education sessions the week before she'd fallen ill.

She looked up. Nate was standing in the doorway, barefooted, wearing the jeans and the plaid shirt he'd had on the night before. He never wore pajamas when they were married, preferring to sleep in his briefs. He was always too hot, she remembered. Sleeping beside Nate was like sleeping next to a warm fire. "Good morning," he said. "You look as if you're contemplating the mysteries of the universe."

His stubble was dark gold against his skin and his short hair was sticking up here and there as though he'd tried to comb through it with his fingers. His shirt wasn't buttoned and the sleeves were rolled up to just below his elbows. His thumbs were hooked into the pockets of his jeans giving her a view of flat stomach and the arrowing line of dark hair that disappeared beneath his waistband. It took a lot of willpower not to let her eyes stray any lower than that. She knew, oh, so well, what lay beneath the much-washed denim, and picturing it made her heart beat so hard and fast she could feel it all the way into her throat.

"Good morning," she replied, striving for a normal everyday tone of voice. "Nothing that momentous, although they say Luther wrote his Ninety-Five Theses while sitting on the toilet. I'm afraid I'm too lazy for anything so philosophical this morning."

"Then you were redecorating my bathroom in your head, weren't you?" One dark winged eyebrow lifted a fraction as he voiced the query.

Sarah felt her face getting red. "No. Not—"

"Liar," he said, with a grin. "I could see the color wheels spinning from here. Quite a challenge what with the 'Age of Aquarius' avocado, don't you agree?"

"It could be done," she said before she could stop herself.

"Want to take on the job when you're back on your feet?" He took a step into the room and the small space became even smaller. She stood up to erase the difference in their heights. Did she want the job? He had asked her what her dreams were the night before but she hadn't answered him. She doubted she would have made sense anyway after their kiss.

She wasn't ready to share her dreams with him, not yet. They were little better than strangers after so much time apart. No matter how willing her body had been to respond to his kiss last night, her heart was still wary.

She had never told a living soul that she hoped someday to have her own decorating and remodeling business. It was only wishful thinking, after all. She was in no position to leave the security of steady employment with HomeContractors and strike out on her own. Not with Matty to raise. But even though she knew it wasn't a practical scenario for their future it hurt to keep denying it.

"No, I don't." The teasing glint in his eyes disappeared and his expression turned remote. She hated to see that happen and rushed to soften her refusal. "I mean you might regret turning me loose on this place. I have expensive tastes."

He tilted his head and looked at her thrift-shop sweat suit. "That's not the way I remember you. Sure, you liked to shop 'till you dropped, but you were a good bargain hunter. 'Never pay full price for anything', wasn't that your motto?"

"I didn't have enough money to pay full price. That's why you should beware if you hire me to redecorate in here. I might be tempted to give my inner diva free reign when you're paying the bills. Eager to change the subject, she said briskly, "C'mon, Matty. Time to get out of the tub. Nate will want to shower and shave."

"Mommy, I go pee pee," Matty said, pointing down at himself, jiggling from one foot to the other. "Now."

"Hang on a second." She spun around. "I'll get your potty chair. I'm sorry, Nate. Can you wait a minute or two more?"

"Take all the time you need." He didn't leave the doorway, resting one shoulder against the frame, his arms crossed over his bare chest.

She pulled the plastic potty seat from inside the vanity where she kept it to try to inconvenience Nate as little as possible, but as soon as he saw it Matty started shaking his head and waving it away. "No. I'm a big boy. Go big boy like Nate."

"Like Nate?" She looked over her shoulder and saw a dark red flush creeping up his neck.

"Uh, we've been practicing. I mean, Matty's been learning how to umm…go pee pee…without his potty chair, right, buddy?"

"Big boy," Matty affirmed pointing down at himself. "I have a ding-a-ling."

Nate's whole face was turning red now. "He doesn't seem to grasp the concept of a closed door." He shrugged. "Anyway, he's old enough. And it will be easier for you not having to lift him on and off the potty chair. Here, I'll help him."

Speechless with surprise at the male bonding that had been going on behind her back, Sarah only nodded and stepped out of his way.

Moving with his usual easy grace, Nate scooped a towel off the rack, lifted Matty out of the tub and dried him with swift, sure strokes. He set Matty on his feet in front of the toilet. He hunkered down so they were almost eye to eye. "Okay, buddy. Remember what I told you, aim careful, ladies don't like having the seat sprayed."

"Right. Watch me, Mommy," he said proudly.

"I am, I am." Sarah put her hand over her mouth to hide a smile, feeling a sharp pang of regret that her baby seemed to be growing up so quickly these past few weeks.

Matty stood on his tiptoes while Nate steadied him with a hand on his shoulder and proceeded to show her his newly acquired skill. When he was done he flushed the toilet and carefully lowered the seat. "See, Mommy. I'm a big boy now," he said, his face shining.

"Yes, you are. And you had an expert teacher."

"It's a survival skill you learn early growing up with three women in the house. Hell hath no fury like a woman who finds the seat's been left up when she didn't expect it."

"Amen." Sarah laughed out loud; she couldn't help herself. Nate joined in and so did Matty, keen to share the joke even if he didn't understand it. "It will be a relief to do away with the potty chair."

"Wash your hands, partner, and then you'd better get dressed," Nate said, draping the towel around Matty's bare shoulders. "Or else your ding-a-ling is going to freeze off and then you'll have to go potty like a girl forever."

"No!" Matty giggled and clutched the towel around him. "I love my ding-a-ling."

That surprised another laugh out of Nate and a giggle out of Sarah. Nate caught her eye in the mirror with a rueful grin. "We all do, buddy."

Nate held Matty up to the sink while he washed

his hands. His easy rapport with her son gave Sarah the courage to make a request of her husband. "Nate, could I ask a favor of you? Could you watch Matty for a couple of hours while I go shopping this afternoon? He needs boots and gloves and a winter hat."

"I thought Dr. Jamison didn't want you to drive until you'd seen her again." Nate set Matty on the floor and tucked the towel snugly round him. "Go get dressed." He gave Matty a pat on the bottom and a push toward the door.

Sarah sidestepped her son and then followed Matty into the hallway. It was hard not to dwell on the feel of Nate's arms around her, the touch of his mouth on hers when they were in such a confined space. "My appointment's Wednesday, I'm sure she'll give me the okay then. I've been off all the medications for over a week. No seizures, no headaches, no dizzy spells. Good as new."

"Uhh, says you."

"Yeah, says me." She hurried around the bed just in time to stop Matty from pulling a drawer out of the bureau onto his bare toes.

"I kind of had other plans," Nate said as she tugged Matty's Spider-Man briefs out of his hand and turned them around the right way. He pulled off his towel and plopped down bare-bottomed on the floor to put them on.

"Oh, I see. That's okay. I can wait a few more

days," she said, hoping her disappointment didn't show. If you didn't count the pumpkin-smashing party, she hadn't been anywhere but Nate's parents' house and her therapy sessions for almost three weeks. Now it looked as if she would be confined to Nate's house for at least a few days more.

"Actually, my plan was we could go out for pancakes and then go on into Adrian. I need to pick up a few things at Wal-Mart and while I'm doing that you can shop for Matty. What do you say?"

"Pancakes." Matty jumped up, one sock half-on, the other dangling from his hand. "Yes. Yes."

A Sunday drive. Breakfast together. Shopping. Family activities. Her family, Nate and Matty, and perhaps, one day a brother or sister for her son. Fantasies even less likely to materialize than the dream of owning her own business. "I don't want to inconvenience you," she said flatly.

Nate came forward and pulled her up by the hands. "I'm asking you to go shopping for a couple of hours, that's all. There are no strings attached. What do you say? I know a little place that serves the best breakfast around. They even make their own sausage. If we don't both waste a lot of time in the shower we can do it all and still be back in time for the kickoff of the Packers-Lions game."

Totally unbidden, the image of the two of them in the shower together flooded her mind with heat and need and pure, unadulterated lust. She jerked her hands from Nate's grasp and fumbled in the drawer for Matty's jeans and sweatshirt. "That sounds great. I can be ready in twenty minutes. You…you shower first and I'll get Matty some cereal. That should hold him over until we get to the restaurant." She looked over her shoulder. "Are you sure you want to do this? Matty's restaurant manners need some work."

"All little kids act up in restaurants. I can't believe he'll be any more of a handful than Becca and I've taken her out for breakfast once or twice. With Joann's boys bouncing off the walls just to make it interesting. I think I can handle it."

"NATE, I WANT TO THROW the ball. C'mon, play with me." Matty was bright-eyed and full of energy. He ought to be, he'd slept all the way back from town. Nate on the other hand wouldn't have minded putting his feet up for awhile, but the look of eagerness on the little boy's face left him unable to say no.

"Okay, you go back for the pass and I'll throw you a bomb." Matty began running toward the creek bank, his legs pumping as fast as they could go. The only problem was that he wasn't looking back over his shoulder. Nate shook his head, still holding the half-size, sponge football he'd bought for Sarah's son at Wal-Mart. "Hey, slow down, pal. You're outrunning my arm."

Matty looked back over his shoulder and promptly fell down, rolling over and over, jumping up again covered with leaves. They were stuck everywhere, on his coat, his hat and gloves and the legs of his pants. "Throw it, Nate. Throw it." He held both arms wide.

Nate pitched the yellow and blue football in a soft lob. The ball hit Matty squarely in the chest and his arms closed around it. He took two stumbling steps and sat down hard still clutching his prize.

Nate was almost as surprised as the little boy. "Well, I'll be darned." He swung around to see if Sarah was watching. She was standing a few feet behind him holding a couple of plastic shopping bags in each hand. "Did you see that? The kid's a natural." He couldn't keep the grin off his face. "He's going to make a heck of a wide receiver one day."

"Wonderful, then maybe he'll get drafted by the pros and he can take care of me in my old age, since thank heaven, it seems I'm going to have one." She chuckled and he joined in. It felt good. They'd laughed together a lot in the early days of their marriage. But the laughter had ended abruptly when they began arguing over Sarah getting pregnant. He found himself shying away from memories of the old days, much preferring the time they were spending together in the here and now.

"It was good of you to buy him the football, Nate."

"It's only a couple of dollars, Sarah, no big deal. Here, let me take those bags." The trouble was he had wanted to buy her son so much more. There had been helmets and miniature shoulder pads to go with the sponge ball. He'd seen a pair of hockey skates, really small ones, and a half-size stick and puck. Matty would be four on his next birthday. He was old enough to learn to skate. They didn't have a ton of snow in this part of Michigan, not like in the north of the state, but they did have plenty of cold weather and the high school had a good rink that had open skating on the weekends. And when it got really cold there was always the pool behind the creek dam, and the lake to skate on.

She was looking at him with a quizzical half smile on her face. "I can carry these."

"I'll take them," he said at the same moment. She sounded a little breathless. Was it because she was tired out? Or was it because they were so close, their hands touching, their breath mingling like smoke in the frosty air? He saw the color in her cheeks, the brightness in her eyes, and didn't think she was over-tired.

"Okay." She thrust the sacks at him as if they were filled with snakes instead of socks and little T-shirts and X-Men underwear. "If we hurry I can get that syrup stain out of your sweater before kickoff." Her words were still breathless and this time he was certain it wasn't because she was tired. He liked the idea of her being off balance when they were so close. He felt the same way. "Matty!" She dropped the plastic bags at his feet and started running.

Nate whirled around just in time to see the little boy disappearing down the steps he'd carved in the creek bank, clutching his ball in one hand, the other barely able to reach the plank railing. "I'll get him," he said passing her before she had gone five yards. He caught up with Matty halfway down the staircase.

"What are you up to, buddy?" he asked, scooping the little boy into his arms.

"Go down there," Matty pointed. "I want to throw my ball in the water."

"Can't do that, bro. It will float out into the lake and we won't be able to get it."

"I want to throw my ball." He squirmed to be set free. "Let me go. I don't want you to hold me."

"Can't let you go, buddy." Nate looked down the steep bank at the small grassy area where the children often played in the summer months. Many years before a huge oak had fallen across the creek that formed the boundary of his property and Harm's, damming up a major portion of the stream and creating a good size pool behind it. For most of the summer the depth of the pool was no more than a foot or two, the water dark and still, but during the spring runoff and after heavy fall rains it was much deeper. Directly behind the oak trunk itself, now mostly sunk in the mud, brush had piled up during the wet weather they'd had over the last couple of weeks. Nate had been promising himself to clean it out before the stream froze so the kids could skate without impaling themselves on broken branches, but he hadn't gotten around to it yet.

"What's wrong?" Sarah had halted on the second step from the top. "Why's Matty crying? Did he fall?"

"Momma." He held out his hands, his face screwed up for a real howl. His ball dropped out of his hands and went bouncing down the steps to the water's edge. He pitched forward from the waist fighting to be let down. Nate grunted in surprise and tightened his hold slightly to keep from dropping him. "I want my momma."

"I told him he couldn't throw his ball in the creek. He didn't like hearing me say it." Nate set Matty on his feet. "Stay put," he commanded, and headed down the last half-dozen steps to get the ball.

Matty obeyed Nate's order but from the mutinous look on his tear-stained face it wouldn't be more than a few seconds before he changed his mind and went charging after him. "I want to throw my ball in the water." He stomped his foot. "Now."

"Matthew David Taylor." The tone of command in Sarah's voice got Nate's attention as well as

Matty's. "You are not going to throw your new ball in the water. That's not what it's for."

"Make it splash. Boom!" Matty threw up his hands to simulate a cascade of water just as he'd seen Jack and Tyler do at the party. "Big splash like the stones!"

Sarah held out her hand as Nate waited at the bottom of the steps watching the battle of wills play out above him. "You don't really want to throw your ball in the lake. It will float away and not come back. That would make you sad."

"No, it wouldn't," he said, but he started reluctantly up the steps toward his mother. "It would make a big splash. I want to make splashes."

"You can do that in the bathtub instead. Tomorrow you can make all the splashes you want."

"In the water. Bathtubs are for girls." He took Sarah's hand, pointedly ignoring Nate trudging up the steps behind them.

"Here's your ball, buddy." He attempted to hand the little boy the football, but Matty batted it out of his hands.

"No! I don't want it. I don't like you." He stuck out his tongue at Nate.

"Matthew. You apologize to Nate right now. You do not stick out your tongue at adults."

"No." He crossed his arms over his chest and stared down at his shoes.

"It's okay, Sarah."

She looked at him and shook her head. "It is not all right for him to behave badly, you know that as well as I do. Matty, if you don't tell Nate you're sorry you'll have to sit in the time-out chair in the bedroom all by yourself."

"Don't care."

"Yes you do. Matthew, we're waiting."

He continued to stare at his shoes for a few moments longer. "Can I watch *Blue's Clues* while I'm in the time-out chair?"

"No."

He lifted his head, his eyes were narrowed, his mouth a tight line. "I'm sorry," he mumbled, refusing to look Nate in the eye.

"That's okay, Matty." Nate didn't add anything else, not sure what he was supposed to say.

"Thank you, Matty," Sarah said. "That's being a good boy."

"I still don't like you." Matty spun around and ran off toward the trailer before anyone could stop him.

"Boy, I sure blew that one. I'm sorry, I shouldn't have tried to discipline him. It wasn't my place."

"Don't be ridiculous, Nate. You did exactly the right thing. Matty's almost four. He's old enough to learn the value of his possessions. And he's certainly old enough to learn what no means."

"I was never around Jack and Ty much at that age

so my experience is pretty limited. And Becca…well, she's a girl." He wished now he'd never bought the football, and forget about the hockey stick and skates. They would probably have gotten him a kick in the shins. He was a bust at this substitute father thing.

"Yes, and I bet all she has to do is bat those long, golden eyelashes and flash you a smile and you'd walk over hot coals to get her cin'mon sweetie." Sarah laughed loudly and freely. "Oh, Nate, listen to yourself. You've led men into combat and dealt with explosives that could bring down a building, and you're letting your confidence get beaten into the ground by a three-year-old's temper tantrum."

He stuck his hands in his pockets and looked down at his shoes much the same way Matty had done. He felt like a fool, but he hadn't realized he would care so much. "You're probably right. But what if it happens again?"

"It will happen again and you'll deal with it the same way we are now, with firmness, love and patience." She stopped and put her hand on his arm so that he stopped, too, and turned to face her. "Do you realize what just happened here?"

"Yeah, I got my butt chewed by a munchkin."

She smiled. "Besides that. Matty made a stand. He stood up for himself. It's the first time since I got sick that I've seen him act like a normal ornery, little boy, not a passive shadow of himself. He's not afraid any more. I have you, and your family to thank for that, for taking him into your hearts and your homes and giving him back his confidence, in himself and our lives. It's a debt I can never repay." She rose on her tiptoes and gave him a little kiss on the cheek. "Thank you, Nate." Her breasts brushed against the sleeve of his coat, her scent enveloped him, her lips were soft as silk against his cold skin.

She left her hand lying on his arm as they began walking again, and when his scattered senses settled back into order, Nate found himself thinking that there were many ways to repay a debt, and as a down payment the kiss would do just fine.

CHAPTER EIGHT

"THE FILMS look very good, Sarah. I think we can safely say you're on the road to a full recovery. I'd like to speak with you and your husband in my office for a few minutes."

Dr. Jamison's last remark startled Sarah slightly. She hadn't expected to have Nate included in a discussion with the surgeon, but on second thought, she should have. Dr. Jamison had no reason to believe their marriage, although hasty, was anything other than genuine. They were walking down the hallway of the busy medical office as she spoke. It was too late to give the other woman an explanation of the complicated circumstances surrounding her marriage—besides, she had no objection to Nate's presence. Perhaps he would feel less responsible for her if he heard the doctor release her with his own ears.

Dr. Jamison opened the door of her office and stepped back so Sarah could precede her. Nate was already there, seated on an upholstered chair in front of the desk. Sarah took a quick look around. The only other time she had been here she had been far too agitated to pay attention to the surroundings. It was a small room with pale walls, wine-colored carpet, and a trio of bookcases behind the desk. To her right a large window overlooked a courtyard that she vaguely remembered having been filled with planters of late-season mums the first time she saw it, but now was as barren and dreary as the November afternoon.

"Mr. Fowler, it's good to see you again," Dr. Jamison said, offering Nate her hand.

"You, too, Doctor." Nate rose to return the greeting. He was wearing a black leather jacket over a dark pullover and dark pants. He stood tall and straight and his demeanor was unmistakably military, even in civilian clothes.

"Please, have a seat."

Nate sat down again and Sarah slid into the chair beside him. Dr. Jamison folded her hands on the top of her desk and regarded them both with a smile. "I just finished telling your wife that the X-rays we took look fine and the progress report from her physical therapist is excellent. Her neuro responses have returned to normal, and I see no reason to believe that my prognosis after the surgery wasn't the correct one. Sarah should recover completely with few, if any, long-term effects of the surgery."

"I am recovered, Dr. Jamison," Sarah interjected.

The surgeon lifted her hand, palm outward as though to slow Sarah's headlong response. "You're well on your way, but fully recovered? No, I'm afraid not quite."

"I feel fine. I'm ready to go back to work." Little twinges of uneasiness began to flutter in Sarah's chest. Why was Dr. Jamison hesitating this way? She was running out of money. She needed to start bringing in a paycheck again. She and Matty couldn't rely on Nate's generosity much longer.

Dr. Jamison opened a folder Sarah hadn't noticed lying on her desk. "You're employed by HomeContractors, correct?" Belatedly Sarah realized the folder must contain her insurance information as well as her medical records.

"Yes." Sarah could feel Nate watching her but she kept her eyes fixed on the surgeon's face. "It's almost time for the holiday rush. I...they need me."

"HomeContractors has a very generous illness and family-leave policy, I believe. You can take up to six months recovery time and still retain your benefits, isn't that right?"

"Yes." It was true, her job would be there for her, but there were no disability payments included in the benefit package, surely the doctor knew that.

"Then I suggest you not return to work until after the first of the year."

"That's almost two months." Sarah's heart sank. She was down to her last few hundred dollars. "I…I can't wait that long. I need the money."

Dr. Jamison's expression was neutral as her gaze moved to Nate's face. Sarah was appalled at what she'd just revealed. Why had she said such a thing? It made it sound as if Nate couldn't support her and Matty even for so short a time.

"Sarah," he said smoothly. "You don't have to rush back to work. We'll do fine without your salary for a couple more months."

She looked at him, trying to convey her apology without speaking. His words had been supportive, showing no indication of embarrassment, but his eyes were dark and reflective, defeating any attempt she might make to read his emotions. Heartsick and embarrassed, she turned back to Dr. Jamison. "Why can't I go back to work?"

"Your job requires lifting and climbing ladders, among other things, doesn't it?"

"Yes, it does." HomeContractor stores were huge, warehouse-like affairs. Many articles were stored on shelving ten or twelve feet off the floor. She was up and down ladders all day long.

Dr. Jamison leaned forward slightly, her tone gentle. "Sarah, your surgery was extensive. We were working very close to your spinal cord. You have a lot of muscle and tissue damage that needs to heal fully. If I thought you'd listen, I would restrict your driving privileges for another month, too." Sarah opened her mouth to object but the surgeon forestalled her. She smiled. "I won't go that far, but please do be careful behind the wheel especially now that the weather is getting bad. I'm sorry if you're disappointed about returning to work but, believe me, this is one of those times when an ounce of prevention really is worth a pound of cure. Taking it easy for a few more weeks now will ensure you won't have back and neck problems, perhaps even migraines, in the future. Surely that's worth the lost income?" She stood up signaling an end to the appointment. As Sarah and Nate rose, she came around the desk and took Sarah's hand in both of hers. "Take my advice, go home and enjoy the holidays, then come back and see me after the first of the year. I promise you I'll write the release slip for you to go back to work then, with no further restrictions or lectures. Agreed?"

A dozen arguments ran through Sarah's brain, but she knew all of them were futile. "Agreed." She manufactured a smile that she hoped didn't look as forced as it felt. "I am very, very grateful for all you've done for me, Doctor."

"No more grateful than I am that it turned out so well." She gave Sarah's hand a squeeze. "Stop by the desk on the way out and make an appointment with the receptionist." She turned to Nate. "I know you'll see she follows my instructions, Mr. Fowler."

"Yes, ma'am, I'll do my best."

She nodded and her smile grew broader. "Good, that's what I wanted to hear. Happy Thanksgiving both of you. Now, if you'll excuse me, I have three more patients to see." Moments later, Sarah and Nate were alone in the hallway.

"I think this is the way out," he said, pointing to the left.

"I'm sorry, Nate. I thought she would release me today. It threw me off guard when she didn't. I…I shouldn't have mentioned money."

"No problem." He put his hand on the small of her back. She didn't want to be that aware of him, not at the moment. She took a step sideways so that he couldn't reach her. He dropped his hand to his side.

"It is a problem and I'm sorry I embarrassed you." She wrapped both hands around the strap of her purse. She needed a winter coat of her own, gloves, a hat and boots, gasoline and snow tires for the minivan. Her car insurance was due the first of December. She hadn't even thought about Christmas gifts for Matty. Even if she charged everything on her credit card, the payments would come due before she had money coming in. The interest would be exorbitant. Add to that her remaining medical bills and what she already owed Nate and it would take her years to get out of debt.

"How about three o'clock on January third?" From the tone of her voice, Sarah realized the heavy-set, middle-aged receptionist behind the front desk had already asked the question more than once.

"Uh, yes. That's fine." Her voice sounded hollow even to her own ears but she couldn't help it. She felt as if she carried the weight of the entire world on her shoulders. The woman scribbled the date and time on an appointment card and handed it to Sarah, who stared unseeingly at the turkeys, pilgrims and pumpkin pies that adorned the woman's colorful lab smock.

She shoved the card into her purse, then headed for the automatic doors to the parking lot without even looking to see if Nate was following.

"Would you like to stop somewhere for an early dinner? I don't get to Ann Arbor often so I can't recommend any place special," he said as they stepped out into a gray, misting drizzle. She shivered. It wasn't even cold enough to snow yet and she felt chilled to the bone. What would it be like when winter really set in?

"I'm not hungry." She waited for him to unlock the passenger door of his truck, then climbed inside. The lump of despair in her throat was so big she didn't think she could swallow a bite, and she certainly couldn't afford an expensive meal, anyway.

Nate glanced at his watch as he put the key in the

ignition. "It's still early. Let's wait until we get back to Adrian to decide where to have dinner."

"Sure. Whatever." She leaned her head against the window watching the play of the windshield wipers across the glass. The morning had been bright and sunny, but halfway to Ann Arbor, a line of dark clouds had appeared on the horizon, and now, late in the afternoon, the day had turned as bleak as her spirits.

Nate didn't say anything more. It was rush hour and he concentrated on his driving. After fifteen minutes or so they left the congestion around the university behind them, then they were outside the city entirely, heading toward home.

Home.

Cottonwood Lake was home now. She'd come to love the rolling Michigan countryside, although today it had little to recommend it, the colors all melting into the grays and browns of early winter. Regardless of her bad mood and the uninviting weather, she knew she wanted to stay, to make a place here for herself and her child. But she didn't want to build that life on a foundation of indebtedness to Nate and his family.

What was she going to do? She closed her eyes but found no inspiration in the darkness behind her eyelids.

"Sarah, wake up." Nate touched her arm, giving her a gentle shake. "We're back in Adrian."

She sat up with a jerk and felt a twinge of pain. Automatically she rubbed the back of her neck.

"You okay?" Nate asked. He had slowed the truck at the intersection of two highways. She looked around and recognized where they were. Her spirits dropped several more degrees. To her left was the clean but shabby motel where she and Matty had stayed those first two frightening weeks after they left Texas. She'd chosen it because it was just down the road from the HomeContractors store. She didn't want to return to the seedy little motel, especially over the holidays, but she might have no choice. She didn't have the money for a security deposit on an apartment now and wouldn't anytime soon.

"I'm fine. I have a crick in my neck, that's all."

"You've been asleep almost an hour. Have you changed your mind about getting something to eat?"

"No," she snapped before she could stop herself. Her sleep hadn't been restful but filled with snatches of nightmare, leaving her more tired than she'd been before she closed her eyes. "I'm not hungry, really."

Ahead of them the lights of Adrian were muted by the rain. "Okay, we'll keep driving, but mind if I pull into the drive-through and get a sandwich?" Nate asked.

"Of course not." She knew she should tell him to stop wherever he chose and she would go inside with him so that he could have a good hot meal, not just a burger from a fast-food joint, but she was just too depressed.

He coasted up to the restaurant drive-through and waited his turn in the silence she'd imposed on them. The radio was tuned to a country station but the volume was too low to make out the words to the song that was playing. Nate placed his order and added a cup of hot chocolate for her.

She opened her mouth to refuse, but he held up his hand in warning. "You don't have to eat anything but you're going to get some hot liquid in you. You're shivering even with the heat turned on full blast. Aren't you feeling well?"

"I'm fine." She could see the hard set of his mouth and the jut of his chin from the corner of her eye and decided it was futile to argue further. She accepted the cup of hot chocolate and blew on the opening in the plastic lid to cool it. He ate his sandwich while he drove, then wadded up the wrapper and sack and tossed it on the floor. The tension between them was so thick it hovered like the fog lying in the hollows of the fields alongside the road.

The turnoff to Cottonwood Lake loomed in the headlights. Nate waited for an eighteen-wheeler to pass from the opposite direction, as it splashed water against the side of the truck with the force of scattershot, then made the turn. Sarah finished her cocoa and sat holding the empty cup. She was still cold, still

shivering. They passed Tessa and Keith's house.
Keith's pickup was parked in the driveway. Tessa had
replaced the Halloween decorations on her front
lawn with an inflatable turkey in a pilgrim hat. The
house was brightly lit, warm and snug against the
wet night. Sarah imagined the three of them sitting
down to dinner, Keith standing at the sink, fixing a
salad, Tessa moving with the ponderous grace of a
very pregnant woman as she set the table, Becca
laughing and dancing around the room safe and secure in her parents' love, and her misery intensified.

They drove up the hill to the barn and parked
under the oak. The lake was an ebony blanket edged
by a fringe of lights. The sky was low and luminous,
gray with rain. Across the lawn she could see Erika
moving around in the kitchen of Nate's trailer. They
had dropped Matty off at Arlene's when they left for
Ann Arbor, but Erika was to have picked him up
after school to bring him home and watch over him
until Sarah's return. She had promised him mac and
cheese and hot dogs for supper and *Shrek 2* afterward. Matty hadn't made a bit of a fuss when she and
Nate drove away, waving happily from Arlene's back
porch. He was comfortable now with all of Nate's
family. She didn't want to uproot him again so soon,
thrust him once more into the care of strangers.

Nate levered the truck into Park and turned sideways on the bench seat so that he was facing her. "All

right, Sarah, what gives? You've been acting strange ever since we left the doctor's office. Are you sure you're not getting sick?"

"I'm sure."

"Then tell me what's wrong."

How many times had he made that demand in the past? The memory made her angry with herself, resentful of him. In the old days he had usually spoken in frustration, sometimes in amused patience. She was too upset to realize that tonight it was neither of those emotions that colored his voice. "All right, I'll tell you what's wrong. I have exactly three hundred and seventeen dollars to my name. My car insurance is due. Christmas is coming. My son and I are essentially homeless. I've shanghaied you into a sham marriage and now you're going to be saddled with us for almost two more months. I don't have enough money to buy a winter coat and I'm damned sure I'm not going to ask you for any more." To her horror the tears she'd worked so hard to suppress through the long stressful weeks of her illness came spilling down her cheeks.

"Sarah, don't cry. Here, take this." He had shrugged out of his coat and was trying to wrap it around her shoulders.

She scooted out of reach but since she was already almost against the door, the withdrawal was largely symbolic. "I'm not crying," she said, scrubbing her hands over her cheeks. "I don't cry anymore, it upsets Matty." She stared out the truck window, blinking hard to banish any more tears before they could fall.

"Sarah, I've told you time and again that money is not a problem."

She turned on him fiercely, her hands balled into fists. "It is to me, Nate. It's a big problem. I'm not the same person you were married to before. I don't want to be taken care of by any man, especially you. I've worked too hard to grow up, to learn to depend on myself, to make a life for me and Matty." But if she was brutally honest with herself, part of her did want Nate to be there for her, to take care of her— and always would. "I don't want to go back to being the helpless, clinging near-child I was when you divorced me," she insisted forcefully, as much to convince herself as him.

"You could have fooled me. Right now a child is exactly what you're acting like. What good will it do you to get pneumonia?" He reached around her and draped his coat over her shoulders and this time she let him. His warmth and scent enveloped her and she couldn't stop herself from snuggling into the soft leather, but only for a moment. She couldn't weaken now, that would be the worst sort of backsliding. He opened the glove box and dragged out a spiral notepad with a pen clipped in the webbing. He flicked on the overhead light and she blinked in the sudden glare. "Here, take this. Figure out what you think you owe me. Add on whatever it'll take to keep the two of you going until you have a paycheck coming in again. However much it is, it's yours. No interest, no time limit. Pay me back whenever you can." She could see his knuckles turn white even in the near darkness.

She took the notebook because she didn't know what else to do with it, appalled at her loss of control. "I'm sorry, Nate. I didn't mean to sound ungrateful."

"You don't owe me a thing, Sarah, but if you feel that trapped, that beholden to me then I won't make you stay a day longer than you want to." He stared straight ahead at the dark rectangle of the barn. Then he surprised her by adding, "I always thought we divorced each other."

She had hurt him with that thoughtless remark, she realized. "I'm sorry. I shouldn't have said that, Nate, but the rest of what I said is true." She couldn't go wobbly now, give in to her almost overwhelming urge to have him take her in his arms and make the rest of the world go away, just like in the old days. The world never did go away. It came back, bigger and badder and more uncertain than before. "I don't want to have to impose on you for two more months. I want to be in charge of my life again."

She clutched the door handle. She needed to get out of the truck, get herself back under control or she would start crying again. "I didn't expect Dr. Jamison to refuse to let me go back to work today. It was like a kick in the stomach. It made me feel weak and helpless again, the way I did when we split up. I'm sorry if you don't want to hear that, Nate, but that's the way it is."

CHAPTER NINE

NATE FROWNED DOWN at the parts manual on the workbench. He'd been staring at the same page for fifteen minutes and still had no idea what he was looking for. His mind was on other things. Frank Heller had called him from Florida. He had a line on a Harley-Davidson 1936 EL. A Knucklehead. The first year Harley had produced the now classic sixty-one engine. Those bikes could do a hundred miles an hour straight out of the crate. How many of them were even in existence anymore? Maybe a hundred? No more than that. The only one he'd known of coming on the market in the last two years had gone for six figures. He'd never worked on a Harley before, but the thought of getting the opportunity was sweet. But he would need a chunk of ready cash to do the job and he'd just offered Sarah whatever she needed, from a bank account that wasn't all that flush.

He understood how important it was for Sarah to feel as if she was in control of her life again if for no other reason than he'd spent three months flat on his back after the accident. But he'd be lying if he said he wasn't happy to hear Dr. Jamison veto her return to work. He agreed with the surgeon that she needed more time to heal—he knew from his own experience just how long it took to get back to one hundred percent. Where he'd made his mistake was thinking that the delay in her return to HomeContractors would guarantee her remaining under his roof, and that's when cool and calm flew out the window.

He slammed shut the parts manual and leaned his palms on the bench. How much longer should he stay out here in the workshop? The whole damned night? He wouldn't freeze but he sure wasn't looking forward to sleeping on Joann's ratty old futon. He'd heard his Uncle Dan's aging F-150 labor up the hill fifteen minutes ago to collect Erika and take her home. Was Sarah in the trailer now, packing to take off into the night? Why had he argued with her about the money? He should have humored her, let her rant and rave and then kissed all her arguments away, cajoled her into his way of thinking just the way he had in the old days.

Except she was right about one thing. She wasn't the same old Sarah and that course of action would have blown up in his face. But was he still the same old Nate? Had he changed enough to give her the space she needed to make her own decision—to stay with him? That's what he really wanted. He just hoped it wasn't too late to plead his case.

He put the manual back on the rack and pulled the plans for the barn renovation out of the drawer. They weren't plans really, not in the sense of an architect's drawing, just sketches a buddy from high school who was a draughtsman had made for him last spring, a wish list more than a blueprint. He sat down on the musty, uncomfortable futon and held them on his lap. The barn wasn't big, not like some of the really massive ones out in the countryside, relics of more than a century ago. It was hip-roofed and compact, built in the early 1900s, used mostly for hay and grain storage, not housing animals. It would take a lot of hard work to refit it into a home but he didn't mind that. And he'd have a lot of help. Gus did carpentry work in the summer, his brother Brandon always needed extra money. He imagined even Harm would want to do his share.

Nate stretched out on the futon, one hand behind his head, the other holding the plans. He'd asked Roger, his old pal, to put all of his wish list in the sketches—granite countertops, a fieldstone fireplace that took up half the north wall and was big enough to roast an ox. He figured he'd have to rebuild the entire foundation to support that kind of weight. He wondered what the estimate on the stonework would be? Was there even a stonemason in the area who would take on the job? Nate closed his eyes, better to keep his mind busy dreaming of a home he might never get around to building than to lie there wondering what Sarah was doing right that moment.

"Nate? Are you asleep?"

"What?" He jerked awake so fast the plans slipped out of his hand and went sailing across the cement floor.

"I'm sorry, I didn't mean to wake you." Sarah was standing over him, his old leather jacket clutched against her breasts with both hands, her eyes wide in the low light, her smile tentative. "I brought you your jacket." She held it out to him.

"I wasn't asleep." But his right arm was. He dragged it out from behind his head and shook it, trying to restore the circulation. He took the jacket and dropped it on the back of the futon. "What time is it?"

She stooped to pick up the scattered papers. "A little after eight. I just got Matty to sleep. I...I thought you might be cold without your jacket. It's nice and warm in here though."

"I put in baseboard electric. I need it warm when I paint."

"Of course. Here, you dropped these." She held out the plans.

"Thanks."

She turned away from him. He rolled the plans into a tube and held it in his hand. He was almost afraid to move for fear he would startle her and she would run away. She walked over to the Four and stood looking down at it. "Is it almost finished?"

He nodded, then realized she couldn't see him with her back to him. "Yes. It needs to be sanded and primed. The painting doesn't take long, but the detailing is time-consuming."

"What color will it be?"

"Indian red," he said, standing up slowly, giving her a wide berth as he moved around the motorcycle, still sitting in the metal cradle he had built to hold it. "And cream. I can't remember right at the moment what the factory name of the color is. They're original, both of them, except the red is more what I'd call maroon or wine. Sort of like the color of Dr. Jamison's carpet today."

She looked up at that. "I'm sorry for the way I acted on the way back from Ann Arbor, Nate. I was angry over the delay on going back to work and I took it out on you."

"I meant what I said about a loan, Sarah. If you're determined to leave I'll give you whatever I can." He half turned and gently tossed the roll of drawings onto the workbench.

She stuck her hands in the pocket of her jacket. "It would be better if Matty and I leave. You'd have your house to yourself again. You'd have your life back."

"What would you do for the next two months?"

She lifted her shoulders. "I don't know. Sit in the motel room and watch TV? I could get a job waiting tables, but then I'd have to put Matty in day care."

"If HomeContractors found out you were working somewhere else while you were on sick leave, wouldn't that jeopardize your benefits? Maybe even your job?"

"Yes."

"Then why leave?"

"Because I want so very badly to stay."

She walked over to the workbench and smoothed out the plans while Nate stayed where he was. "This is your dream, isn't it?" she asked softly.

"One of them."

"I didn't tell you mine when you asked that night after the party. Can I tell you now?" she asked, still without looking at him.

"I would be honored if you did."

She didn't say anything for so long he thought she might have changed her mind and the icy grip that had eased ever so slightly, tightened again. "I like this layout. You've got a good traffic pattern here. The master suite on top of the two downstairs bedrooms leaves the view out over the lake completely unobstructed. The kitchen arrangement needs some work, but it's not a bad design for a guy."

"Hey, I resent that. I spent a lot of time coming

up with that. I watch the Food Channel. I know what I'm doing." He ignored the tightness in his chest, fought to keep the anxiety out of his voice. If she needed a little more time to work up her courage to confide in him, he'd give it to her.

She laughed and he saw the tension in her shoulders relax ever so slightly. She was having trouble keeping the drawings from rolling back on themselves. He came a couple of steps closer and put his hand on the paper to hold it down. She shook her head. "That wasn't very tactful of me, was it? The fireplace is magnificent, but it's going to be a major expense, you know that, don't you?"

"Does it have to go?" She was studying the plans intently, her head cocked a little to the left so that he could see her profile and the silken sweep of her lashes against her cheek. She reached up and pushed her hair behind her ear and he had to stop himself from leaning down to kiss the smooth skin behind it.

"No, not if you're open to suggestions for alternatives."

"Go ahead."

"Well, there are a couple of ways we could go about it. A stone facing and a state-of-the-art metal firebox would reduce the weight load on the foundation by a substantial degree. You don't really need the outside chimney to be stone. It's out of keeping with the rest of the exterior. The siding's not in the best of shape, you know."

"I know."

"They make wonderfully authentic looking vinyl siding that resembles handmade shingles. It would look great—" She tilted her head a little farther to the left and looked up at him. "You're laughing at me," she said, but she didn't sound angry, just a little sheepish.

"No, I'm not. But I do admit I'm having a little trouble picturing you with a hard hat and a tool belt and a pipe wrench in your hand."

"I guess you would if you only remember me the way I used to be."

"Believe me," Nate said quietly. "I almost never think of you the way you used to be anymore."

She accepted the compliment with a gracious nod, and he thought he saw a faint flush of pleased color rise in her cheeks, but he couldn't be sure, not in the dim light of the workshop. "That's my dream, Nate," she said after a few seconds of silence. "I want to start my own business. I can paint and wallpaper. I can do light electrical and plumbing, day-to-day mainte- nance. Maybe someday I could branch out into gen- eral contracting, but that's a long way in the future."

It was almost the last thing he'd expected her to say, although as he thought about it he realized it shouldn't have been. She'd always loved color and shape and texture. He just hadn't imagined she had such a practical bent. Plumbing and electrical. He kept his amusement, and his admiration, to himself. "Cottonwood Lake could use a business like that. Most of the houses around here have been in the same hands since the fifties. Their owners are getting on in years, and they're starting to need help with those kinds of projects. There's quite a bit of gentrification going on, too. Mostly on the other side of the lake, but it's working its way in this direction, no matter how much Granddad grumbles about the yuppies from the university ruining the neighborhood."

A smile had bloomed on her lips as he spoke, but slowly it faded away and he thought he must know what it would feel like to be the last man alive on earth to see the sun go out. "I know," she sighed. She waved her hands over the plans. "It's all just a dream, Nate. Now my first responsibility is raising my son. The best way to do that is to keep my job at Home-Contractors." She rolled up the plans and picked up the architect's tube he stored them in.

Nate folded his hands across his chest and leaned his hip against the workbench. "How badly do you want that dream, Sarah?"

How badly? As much as she'd wanted anything in her life. Or at least she had felt that way until her illness. "It's not a question of how much I want it. It's just not feasible right now." It was what she'd told herself over and over again. Saying it aloud helped reinforce it.

"It might come true more quickly if we stayed together." She stopped with the drawings halfway back in the tube.

"What do you mean, Nate?"

"I mean, why not stay here, on Cottonwood Lake, settle in, get to know people? The bank Joann works for does a lot of small business loans. You may be able to realize your dream sooner than you think."

"I still don't have any money, Nate. Where do you suggest Matty and I live?"

"With me. Stay, Sarah."

"I don't think that's wise, Nate." He didn't move toward her and she was grateful for that. It was growing more difficult to deny how much she wanted to be in his arms, surrounded by his love. With each and every day that passed it grew harder to compare the man he was now with the brash and impatient young sergeant who had wooed her and won her, and then marginalized her in his life.

"It will be good for Matty. Has he ever really had you to himself like this past few weeks?"

He knew that argument would resonate. It made her heart ache to think of returning her son to the care of strangers, as she had had to do since he was six weeks old. "This marriage was never supposed to last, Nate."

He leaned closer. She could smell his aftershave, clean and woodsy, and beneath that the even more intoxicating scent of Nate himself. "I know that and I swear to you it won't last a day longer than you want it to. But there's still something between us, Sarah. Maybe we deserve to see what it is." He slid his hand around her shoulders, cupped the back of her head in his big palm and kissed her. The years and the heartache melted away and she never wanted the moment to end. She slipped her arms around his neck and let him pull her close. There was nothing tentative about their kiss. It was as if her body remembered everything that her conscious mind denied. His taste, his touch, the hardness of his body against the softness of her. Heat pooled inside and spread through her, running like a lava flow beneath her skin. She had never felt more alive, or more afraid.

She put her hands between them and pushed at the hard wall of his chest. He lifted his mouth, but didn't drop his arms. "I'm not asking for anything you aren't ready for, Sarah. I haven't forgotten the bad times, either. But maybe we should give ourselves the chance to move past them."

"I…I'm not ready for this." Panic doused the desire that had come rushing out of nowhere to nearly overpower her. He released her slowly, reluctantly, and she looked up into his face, saw the naked hurt and longing he did nothing to hide. She spoke before her defenses could slam back into place. "I'm not ready for this, Nate." She traced the line of his jaw with the tip of her finger. "But I'm not ready to walk away. We'll stay, at least for a little while."

CHAPTER TEN

"I CAN'T TELL YOU how happy I'll be to drop this kid," Tessa grumbled, one hand on the back of Arlene's kitchen chair, one on the tabletop as she lowered herself heavily onto the seat. "I feel like an elephant and I look like one, too." Sarah, Arlene, Joann and Tessa, along with Nate's brother, Brandon, were all gathered in Arlene's kitchen to wash the mountain of dirty dishes left after Thanksgiving dinner.

"I lost the toss so I'm doing dishes instead of watching the game, but no one told me I had to listen to gross pregnancy talk," Brandon grumbled, making a disgusted face as he caught Sarah's eye.

"You don't look like an elephant. Maybe a hippopotamus, but not an elephant," Joann snickered.

Tessa raised her eyebrows and stared pointedly at the bowl of mashed potatoes covered in turkey gravy that her sister was devouring. "At the rate you're going, you'll be bigger than I am by Christmas."

Joann was wearing slim black pants and a bulky pine-green sweater that effectively hid any early evidence of her pregnancy. "I can't help it. I'm starving all the time. And not one minute of morning sickness to get rid of any of the extra calories, either." As if to underscore her words she took another bite, and sighed blissfully. "I'll worry about losing weight next summer. Now I'm going to enjoy my food."

"I'm not going to think about eating again for at least a week," Arlene announced as she closed the door on the dishwasher and turned around. "Sarah, that platter is far too heavy for you to lift." Sarah pulled her hand back from the huge ironstone turkey plate she'd been about to dry.

"It isn't too heavy, really."

"Brandon will take care of it."

"Hey, I'm in dishwater up to my elbows." He had driven up in a ramshackle old Chevy a few minutes after Nate and Sarah had arrived at Tom and Arlene's for Thanksgiving dinner. He had changed a great deal since Sarah had last seen him. Then he'd been eighteen, a high school senior, and skinny as a rail fence. Now, at twenty-three, he was no longer gawky and tongue-tied, but broad-shouldered and slim-hipped, working on a master's degree in computer science at Purdue. He was the spitting image of Nate when she'd first met him, she had realized with a little shock of surprise. He had greeted her with easy familiarity, behaving as though the return of a divorced daughter-in-law and her fatherless son to the family through a marriage of convenience was an everyday occurrence.

It had been a large and noisy family group gathered around Arlene's cherry dining table, with the overflow accommodated in the kitchen and on card tables in the foyer. Sarah had felt self-conscious at first but soon lost her nervousness because there was simply too much to do. She carried dishes to the sideboard and helped set out plates and cups and silverware, buffet style. She filled the cream pitcher, made sure the little ones had napkins, and that Becca and Matty had sippy cups so the meal wouldn't be interrupted by spilled milk on the carpet. She was part of the appreciative audience that watched Tom carve the huge, golden brown turkey, and joined hands with Nate and Matty in a circle of prayer, offering up her own thanks for the blessings of health and renewed hope in the future that God had granted her and her son.

It was the kind of Thanksgiving she had dreamed about all through her lonely childhood, but had never, even during her first marriage to Nate, experienced firsthand. She didn't allow herself to think that this was probably the only large family gathering she would ever share.

"You can go ahead and dry it," Brandon told her with a wink and a grin as she focused once more on what was going on around her. "It's not a family heirloom. Mom bought it at a flea market a couple of years ago. You won't be cursed if you drop it or anything."

"As far as I'm concerned the best thing Mom ever did is leave her good china in the cabinet during family dinners," Joann said around a mouthful of potatoes and gravy. "I used to worry constantly that the boys would break something, or a piece of Great-Grandma Fowler's silver would end up down the garbage disposal."

"Or disappear like the year the pickle tongs went missing and Mom made me go through two big bags of trash with my bare hands until I found them." Brandon shuddered with great exaggeration. "One of the most traumatic experiences of my childhood. I still can't eat cranberry sauce without remembering the horror of it all."

"Everything was traumatic for you. You were such a little mamma's boy," Tessa teased, moving across the kitchen to give him a quick hug.

"Maybe that's because you were an evil big sister, making my life miserable." Tessa followed up the hug with a punch on the arm. "Ouch, Mom she's hitting me," Brandon whined.

"I was just trying to toughen you up for kindergarten."

"You were trying to destroy me. At least until I got bigger than you and started fighting back." Brandon pretended to lunge at her with soapy hands formed into claws.

Tessa squealed and hopped back a step, her hand on her swollen belly. "Watch it, little brother. I might go into labor right here and now."

"Stop that, you two. It's as though you regress fifteen years the minute you step into this house," Arlene said, shaking her head. "Sarah, I told you to let Brandon dry that." She made clucking sounds with her tongue and reached for the heavy platter. "Oh, well, it's done now. Give it to me. I'll set it in the pantry and Tom can put it away later."

While Sarah handed Arlene the platter, Tessa pulled a dish towel from a cabinet drawer. "Let me finish drying the dishes, Sarah. I'm too uncomfortable to sit, anyway."

"I don't mind, really. There are only a few left."

"Better let her do them, Tessa. Your fingers are like sausages. If you break Grandma Riley's crystal compote, Mom will never forgive you," Joann warned her sister.

Tessa looked down at her ringless fingers. "You've got a point. I don't know why we keep on using the compote when everything else is under lock and key?"

"Because I did not spend three hours making authentic English trifle to serve it in Tupperware," Arlene said, bustling back into the kitchen. It was a big room at the back of the 1920s Craftsman-style bungalow that sat in the middle of a double lot three blocks from Tessa's house on Lake Shore Drive. Joann and Gus lived a mile or two away, along the state highway leading to Hillsdale, but they were keeping their eyes open for a place on this side of the lake.

The kitchen faced east, and filled with morning sunlight and summer bird song, Sarah recalled. The cabinets were floor to ceiling, native walnut with most of their original glass handles. Along with the wall of windows that looked out over the garden, they were the room's best feature. Sarah would have loved to be able refinish them, and next on her imaginary to do list would be tearing up the vinyl tiles because she was certain she'd find oak hardwood underneath that matched the floors in the rest of the house.

"Anyone want a cup of coffee?" Arlene asked. "I'll brew another pot."

"I'm giving up coffee for the duration," Joann said.

Tessa shook her head. "All I do is pee as it is."

"Sarah? How about you?"

"Thanks, I would like a cup."

"Is there any pumpkin pie left?" Ty asked, appearing in the doorway that led to the dining room.

"We haven't even got the dishes done. You can't be hungry already."

He eyed his mother skeptically. "You're eating."

Joann didn't have an answer for that.

"Go play," Arlene said, making shooing motions with her hands. "Get some exercise. It's supposed to start snowing before dark. You can have pie later. What are the other kids doing?"

"Jack's watching football with Grandpa Tom and the guys. Aunt Celeste and Uncle Dan went for a walk. Grandpa Harm is taking a nap. Erika and the little kids are looking at photo albums."

"Any pie left?" Nate appeared in the doorway behind Ty.

"Not you, too," Arlene said.

"What?" Nate asked, feigning innocence. "I'm a growing boy. I'm hungry."

"No you're not. I'm saving that last pie for supper tomorrow and you know it."

"Black Friday supper is a tradition, too," Tessa added. Black Friday had gotten its nickname as the day after Thanksgiving when most retailers began to realize a profit for the year, Joann confided to Sarah.

"Ty, go get your football and Nate can toss us a few," Brandon offered.

"You're not done with the roaster," his mother pointed out.

"It needs to soak. Besides, I'm trying to keep these two away from the pie." He rested his hands on Arlene's shoulders and kissed the top of her head.

"Cut me some slack. Remember, I had an invitation to spend Thanksgiving in Florida."

"And if you'd gone I would have written you out of my will first thing tomorrow morning," Arlene shot back, but she was smiling. "Go on, I'll work on the roaster later."

"Come, my brothers, let's split before Simon Legree here thinks of something else for her kitchen slave to do." The trio grabbed their coats from where they were piled on top of the washer and dryer on the back porch, and headed out into the cloudy November afternoon.

"Thanks for distracting Ty, Mom. Gus and I haven't told the boys about the new baby yet," Joann explained to Sarah. She scraped the last of the mashed potatoes out of her bowl and licked the spoon. "Waiting seven months is an eternity when you're their age."

"Like I said, by Christmas you'll be in maternity clothes. The whole world will know," Tessa remarked.

"Very funny."

Arlene filled two mugs with coffee and slid into the chair beside Sarah's. "Next year I'm going to make reservations for all of us at the yacht club. Marjean Robinson says the buffet is excellent. And there won't be any dishes to do."

"Or any leftovers for after shopping on Friday," Joann said, feigning horror at the thought.

"You say that every year, Mom," Tessa said. "And every year you change your mind."

"This time I mean it."

"Yeah, yeah." Tessa grinned. "What time do you want to leave to go to the mall tomorrow? I want to get as much done as I can. This fellow's getting impatient. I don't think he'll wait for New Year's Eve." She patted her stomach and Sarah's eyes were drawn to the faint movements under her woven smock. "See what I mean?"

"Nothing will get me into the stores on the day after Thanksgiving." Arlene shuddered. "The last time I did that was the year you both insisted on Cabbage Patch Kids and I had to fight off three other desperate mothers to get to the checkout. The very memory makes me want to grab the brandy bottle and top off my coffee. Besides I have a policy to write up tomorrow—the clients want to close on their new house by the end of the month."

Joann and Tessa exchanged looks. "Sarah, why don't you come with us?" Tessa asked, with a welcoming smile. "There are some great sales advertised."

Sarah swallowed against a sudden catch in her throat. They were including her as if she was indeed once again a member of the family. She hated to turn down an invitation from Nate's sisters, especially one that was so obviously meant as an overture of friendship.

"Thanks, but I'm afraid I'll have to pass—" Sarah began with genuine regret, only to be interrupted by the return of the football-tossing trio of Nate, Ty and Brandon.

"We're going to get the rest of the guys and have a real game," Brandon explained as Ty thundered through the kitchen into the dining room and the living room beyond to recruit extra players from the ranks of his male relatives. Brandon handed Nate the football and went to get a glass of water at the sink.

"Do you have other plans?" Tessa asked, ignoring the interruption.

"No. But I don't have anyone to watch Matty."

"He's welcome to stay with me," Arlene said, but she didn't sound too enthusiastic. Sarah didn't blame her. Her mother-in-law looked tired. She had been preparing for the holiday all week and she had already said she would be busy on Friday.

"What's up tomorrow?" Nate asked. He had been standing with one hip propped against the counter, passing the football back and forth between his big, sure hands as he waited for the other men to join him. He was wearing his canvas jacket unzipped, over a heather green chambray shirt that was open at the throat, exposing a triangle of bronzed skin dusted with hair. Sarah's mouth went dry and her stomach tightened with desire as she remembered what it felt like to kiss him there.

"We want Sarah to come shopping with us but she hasn't got a sitter for Matty. Mom's busy and Erika won't be around." Erika and her parents were leaving the next morning for Camp Lejeune in North Carolina where their son, Garland, a Marine, was stationed. They were planning to be gone a week and they were taking Harm with them to visit his grandson.

"I'll keep Matty," Nate said quietly. "He's comfortable with me."

"You have work to do on the Indian."

Nate caught her gaze and held it with the force of his. "Go shopping, Sarah. Buy the coat you've been wanting. This weather won't hold more than another day or two. Matty and I will get along just fine."

Sarah could feel the other women's eyes on her. They had opened their family circle to her and she wanted so badly to step inside. But with each short November day that passed, Sarah was more and more convinced that she had made a dreadful mistake agreeing to stay with Nate. She was beginning to care too much—about his family, about Cottonwood Lake, about him again. She feared great heartache was in store for them both.

"Excellent," Tessa decreed, before Sarah could find the courage to refuse Nate's generous offer. "Then it's settled. We'll pick you up at six."

"Six a.m.?" Sarah hadn't expected that.

"Sure. The Door Buster specials, ya know."

"Mommy! Look!" Matty and Becca came running into the kitchen with Erika close on their heels.

"What is it, honey? What have you got there?"

"Nate," he said, beaming, and thrust a big photo album into her lap. "Nate is G.I. Joe." Matty adored his G.I. Joe doll. He carried it practically everywhere he went.

"Nate was a real soldier. G.I. Joe is a doll." Sarah sat the album on the tabletop and opened the pages. Several years of the Fowlers' lives, before she had married Nate, were laid out before her. There were pictures of Tessa and Joann as young brides. Gus had more hair, and Keith was thinner. A gap-toothed Brandon posing with Nate in his class As, corporal's stripes on his shoulders, Tom and Harm smiling in the background of the snapshot.

Ty came pounding back into the kitchen. "Uncle Nate, help me get my Dad and Uncle Keith up off the couch." He spied the album. "Hey, what's that? Old pictures? Let me see."

There was no shiver of uneasiness, no siren going off in her head to warn Sarah not to turn the page. She flipped it over and there was her past staring her in the face. Snapshots of her and Nate taken the summer they'd spent his two-week leave on Cottonwood Lake. Pictures of them happy and in love, swimming, picnicking, sitting arm in arm, on the steps of

Arlene and Tom's house, her head resting on his shoulder, stars in her eyes and happiness in his smile. Beside it was a snapshot of her in his arms on the dock at Harm's place, her mouth open in a silent scream as Nate threatened to throw her in the water. Always smiling, always laughing. In love for ever and ever.

She had thought she had everything she'd ever wanted in those days. Everything except children, and sadly, children were the one thing Nate wouldn't give her.

"Momma. That's you," Matty said, pointing to one of the pictures.

"Yeah, it is."

Ty leaned closer. Nate stopped passing the football back and forth between his hands and stood very still. All the adults were suddenly silent, frozen in place. "You and Nate. And it's in the summer. You're wearing a bathing suit. How's that? You only came here in October?"

"Ty," Joann cautioned, but he wasn't listening.

"And these are old pictures. Look, there's Erika and she's only little, like Jack." He looked at his mother, then at Arlene, then at Sarah. "I don't get it."

Joann's face was flushed. "I'm sorry, Sarah. I never thought to explain—"

"It's all right, Joann," Sarah said. "Nate and I were married once before, Ty," she said, searching for words to make the complicated situation understandable to a nine-year-old. "That's why I came here to ask for his help when I got sick. Because I knew he…all of you, would take good care of Matty if I couldn't any longer."

"You were married to Nate once before? Cool," Ty said, accepting the explanation easily enough. And then with a child's devastating candor, "Why did you divorce him?"

Sarah took a moment to form her answer. "We hurt each other," she said carefully. "And we decided it was better if we didn't live together anymore."

Ty nodded sagely. "That happens. But you married someone else and had Matty, didn't you?"

"Yes." She pulled Matty close for a hug, not quite daring to meet the eyes of any of the other adults. "I did."

"But Nate didn't marry anyone else, right?" He turned and looked at Nate over his shoulder.

"Right," Nate said, his voice steady. His expression would be steady, too, she knew without looking at him. "I didn't marry anyone else."

"Are you going to stay married to Nate this time?"

"I…I don't know." She saw sadness and uncertainty in Tessa's eyes, knew it would be reflected in Joann's, in Arlene's. She understood Nate's sisters and mother were anxious to learn where their sham marriage was headed, when it would end, but they had avoided asking her. She knew they were worried about Nate's future happiness, and how her leaving again would affect him, but they had refrained from interference of any kind and she was grateful to them for that.

"Well, if you two do stay married it's okay with me." Ty spun around and motioned for Nate to toss him the football. "Let's go back outside, okay."

"Sure." Nate's eyes swept over Sarah's face, but as was so often the case she couldn't read the emotions hidden in their gray depths. He tossed Ty the football but didn't follow him out the door.

"I'm sorry," Erika whispered. "I forgot the little ones didn't know," she gestured helplessly toward the pictures.

"It's not your fault." Sarah hoped her smile looked more natural than it felt. "The subject was bound to come up sooner or later."

"I'll put the album away."

"No!" Matty slammed both hands down on the album to keep Erika from taking it. "I want to look."

Sarah hadn't been paying attention to Matty during the awkward exchange with Ty. He was busy perusing the photos, devouring the pictures of her and Nate together. Then there were no more pictures of her, the family had closed ranks again. The last page of the album contained several shots of Nate with a newborn in his arms.

"Becca's baptism," Tessa murmured, noticing where Matty's attention was directed. "Nate's her godfather." It would have been taken just before Nate shipped out to Afghanistan, the few days leave he'd had after they'd split up for good.

Matty wasn't interested in the adults' talk. "That's me," he said gleefully, pointing to the baby in Nate's arms. "That's me."

"No, honey. That's Becca," Sarah said, patiently.

"No." He spoke more loudly, more emphatically. "Me. Matty. Nate and me." His next question hit Sarah with the force of a blow. "Is Nate my Daddy?"

"No, honey, he's not." Nate hadn't moved from where he was standing. She could feel his eyes on her. "Your daddy was David Taylor. You're named after him, remember?" Sarah's stomach clenched. She knew where this was headed. She had prayed for Nate to love her son during those terrible days and weeks when she was convinced that she would die. She had hoped that Matty would someday feel the same way about the man who had so selflessly agreed to raise him as his own. It seemed she had her wish, now that it was no longer the best thing for either Nate or her son.

"No." He pointed a finger at Nate and broke into a beaming smile that sent shards of bittersweet pain deep into Sarah's heart. "I want Nate to be my dad."

CHAPTER ELEVEN

NATE LAID the back fender of the Four on the workbench and looked over his shoulder at Sarah's son. Matty was sitting cross-legged on the floor on a scrap of indoor-outdoor carpet Nate had scrounged from Harm, banging a big, flat-headed nail into a piece of wood with a tack hammer.

"Bang, bang, bang," Matty chanted as each blow fell. He was wearing the Michigan hat Jack had given him and Nate noticed his blond hair was sticking out around his ears.

"You're getting a little shaggy looking there, buddy. I'll take you to the barber with me when I go next week." If Sarah okayed the trip. Technically he was Matty's stepfather, but he really had no say in how Sarah raised her son, even concerning something as insignificant as a haircut.

"Bang, bang, bang," Matty repeated, his tongue tucked in the corner of his mouth. "Really big bang."

Maybe a hammer and nails weren't the greatest toys in the world but as long as he didn't smash his thumb or drop the hammer on his foot Nate guessed it was okay to let him pound away. Like mother, like son, he could always say if Sarah demanded to know why Matty was playing with real tools, and not plastic or wooden replicas.

"I need more," Matty announced, although the hammering didn't stop.

Nate turned around. Matty had pounded the nail all the way into the wood and then some, leaving an impressive dent in the soft pine.

"Here you go." He opened one of the old baby-food jars he used to store nails and screws, and dropped to his haunches with a smothered groan. His knee and ankle were aching like the devil today. A cold front had moved through during the night and this morning they had awakened to their first real snow.

"Matty's never seen snow," Sarah had said early that morning as she peered out the kitchen window. She was already dressed and waiting for Tessa and Joann to pick her up for their shopping spree. "Look, it's still coming down. Do you think there will be enough to make a snowman this afternoon?" She'd looked like a little kid seeing her own first snowfall, her cheeks flushed, her eyes sparkling with excitement. "I'll buy him a pair of boots and a heavier pair of mittens so he can play outdoors. Thanks for offering to watch him for me, Nate."

"Sarah, he's my stepson now. Looking after him is part of the job description, remember." He'd never referred to himself as Matty's stepfather before, but yesterday in his parents' kitchen when the little boy had pronounced him his father Nate had decided the time had come.

He'd braced himself for her to reopen the argument about her and Matty finding a place of their own before the end of the year, but lucky for him Joann and Tessa had driven up at that very moment and honked the horn. "You'd better go," he'd said with a smile. "Hell hath no fury like my sisters if they're not the first ones through the doors when the mall opens after Thanksgiving."

And so it came to pass that a few hours later it was, he, Nate Fowler, a man who would never father a child of his own, who got to show Sarah's son the wonder of his first snowfall, to show him how to catch snowflakes on his tongue, and to fall on his back, scissoring his arms and legs to make snow angels. He'd enjoyed every minute of it. The only thing that would have made it better was if Sarah had been there to share in the experience, the three of them the family he wanted them to be.

"Nate. I want to pound some more." Matty's tone was impatient. Nate suspected it wasn't the last time he'd voice the demand. He pulled another nail out of his pocket and steadied it for the little boy. Matty took careful aim and hit the nail right on the head.

"Good job," he praised. "You keep practicing and before you know it you'll be as good as your mom." He fashioned a mental image of Sarah with a tool belt around her slim waist, hammer in hand, as she worked away on a project. Maybe he would buy her an automatic nail gun for Christmas. Would that be an appropriate gift? Somehow he doubted his sisters would give it their seal of approval, but he wasn't going to make the mistake of buying her anything too intimate, or personal. Perhaps for her birthday in the spring…if they were still together.

Hell, there he went again anticipating the worst instead of planning how to get what he wanted. Sarah in his arms, in his bed, in his life—forever this time. Maybe he'd buy her the nail gun after all and wrap it up with some of the perfume she always wore. It had a soft, lemony fragrance and the bottle that sat on the shelf on her side of the bathroom sink was nearly empty. Perfume and a nail gun. Was that covering all his bases or what?

Nate glanced at his watch. Almost one o'clock. He wondered if he could put Matty down for his nap and then come back to wet sand the fender? He was just about ready to start painting the Four. He glanced over at the bike. She was starting to look good. The chrome handlebars and exhaust pipe reflected the light so brightly it hurt your eyes, while the nickel engine bolts shone with a softer glow and the frame gleamed darkly, looking like nothing so much as a black tether anchoring the streamlined Indian to the ground. He rubbed his hand over the leather seat, original, just like everything else on the bike. The parts he couldn't repair or rebuild he'd fabricated himself. The painting and detailing would take him most of next week, but the motorcycle would be ready to ship off to Detroit ahead of the deadline. A complete rebuild and restoration like this one took months, but in the end it was worth it. He'd never get rich but he could make a good living—for him and his family.

"More nails," Matty demanded.

"Later, buddy. It's time to go up to the trailer and take your nap."

"No nap." Matty dropped his hammer and crossed his arms over his chest. "Not sleepy."

"Too bad." Nate levered himself up off the floor with one hand, then reached down and scooped the little boy into his arms. Matty wiggled and flopped over his arm and demanded to be put down. "Nope," Nate said firmly. He set Matty on the workbench and reached for his coat. "Nap time. And then we'll come back out here and you can pound some more nails."

"No," Matty wailed, but he quit struggling. "Are you going to take a nap, too?"

"I'm going to make some phone calls and start lining up some of the parts I need to make another motorcycle." Joann had called late Wednesday afternoon to tell him his loan application had been approved. She'd wired the money through to Frank Heller before she left the bank. His old boss and the EL were due to roll into Cottonwood Lake sometime before Christmas.

"Here, put your coat on." Nate held the little Lions coat up by the collar and motioned for Matty to put his arms in the sleeves.

Matty did as he was told but he wasn't quite ready to give up the fight. "Can I play in the snow?" he asked as Nate zipped it up.

"After your nap your mom will be home and she'll play in the snow with you."

"I'm not sleepy," Matty insisted stubbornly. "I want to play in the snow."

"You don't have to go to sleep. You can watch a SpongeBob tape if you want to," Nate said, ignoring the demand to play outside. He was getting the hang of dealing with an almost-four-year-old. You avoided telling them "no" straight out, and if you had enough patience you could usually move them in the direction you wanted by other routes.

"Clifford, not SpongeBob," Matty said.

"Clifford, the Big Red Dog, it is."

Twenty minutes later Nate stuck his head in the

bedroom door and was pleased to see Matty asleep, his thumb in his mouth. He'd arranged the sponge football that had caused the uproar down by the creek ten days earlier, and his G.I. Joe on the pillow beside him. His left arm was wrapped around the ratty old blanket he'd carried everywhere the first couple of weeks after he and Sarah arrived, but now seemed only to need when he was going to sleep.

Nate walked as quietly as his heavy work boots would allow back to the kitchen and sat down at the table to look through the specs manual on the EL that had arrived in the mail that morning. The bike was a beauty, the engine design so efficient a version of it was still in production after nearly seventy years. Harleys were fantastic bikes and he was looking forward to the challenge of restoring the Knucklehead, but his heart still belonged to his Indians.

He propped his aching leg up on the banquette and leaned his head back against the wall. He'd spent a restless night unable to find a comfortable position on the narrow bunk bed. He'd just close his eyes for a minute or two to rest them. It was probably the leftover turkey sandwich he'd had for lunch that was making him sleepy. It sure couldn't be the small print in the handbook. He was only thirty-four, he couldn't need reading glasses already.

The sound of the back door of the trailer slamming shut jerked Nate awake with his heart pound-

ing, the same way it used to do back in Iraq when
the bad guys lobbed a mortar shell into the com-
pound. He looked at the clock on the microwave
above the stove. He hadn't been asleep more than
five minutes. He came up off the seat in one swift
move. He might have dozed off but his mind was
wide awake. Sarah wasn't due back for a couple of
hours. The sound of the door closing could mean
only one thing. Matty had woken up and gone outside on his own.

Nate reached out with one arm and grabbed his
coat off the back of the banquette as he bolted down
the narrow hallway of the trailer. He stuck his head
through the bedroom door. Sure enough the bed was
empty and Matty and his sponge ball were gone. He
opened the back door of the trailer, spotted the little
shoe prints immediately and knew with a terrible
certainty where Matty was headed. He couldn't spare
even the few seconds it would take to go back and
get Matty's coat. "Damn," Nate said under his breath
and took off in a limping run. The sight that greeted
him at the top of the creek steps chilled his blood.

Matty was crawling out onto the half-buried trunk
of the old oak. His football floated just out of his
reach, caught up in the snarl of brush that Nate still
hadn't found time to clear out of the stream. He
started warily down the snow-slick wooden risers,
cursing his uncooperative knee with every step.

"Matty. Partner, stay put. Let me get your ball for you," he said, trying not to let the fear that gripped him seep into his voice. The last thing he wanted was to startle the little boy and send him tumbling into the water.

"My ball." Matty turned his head toward Nate. His eyes were huge with terror and his mouth trembled. "I don't like it here."

"I'll come and get you. Don't move, okay?"

"Okay." There was little purchase for Matty's fingers, however. High water had long ago scoured away the tree's bark, leaving the trunk smooth and slippery.

Nate took a careful step onto the trunk, then realized even if he made it the twenty feet or so to where Matty was crouched it would be impossible for him to pick up the little boy and carry him back the way he had come. The trunk simply wasn't wide enough for him to turn around on it without risking both of them falling headlong into the water. Crawling along the trunk wasn't an option because, once he reached Matty, he still wouldn't be able to turn around. His only other recourse was to wade into the creek and carry Matty back that way. With the rain they'd had over the past few days Nate figured the water behind the makeshift dam was at most about four feet deep. As long as he didn't step in a washout and end up in over his head he should be all right.

"Hang on, buddy." Nate stepped off the bank, shoes and all. He didn't want to waste time unlacing the heavy, steel-toed work boots. There wasn't a lot of current in the creek at this point, but the water was dark and silt-filled with the runoff from farm fields along its course. If Matty slipped off the log and went under—Nate refused to let himself finish the dark thought.

In two steps he was in water up to his thighs. It was so cold he felt as if his skin was on fire. The dull ache in his bad leg increased tenfold. He gritted his teeth and kept on wading. He'd entered the creek on the side of the dam where the water was deepest, but the bank on the downside of the oak was steep and muddy. He hadn't trusted his weak leg to make the climb up or down. But what he couldn't see until he was already in the water was that the brush piled up against the dam was really the top of a small tree, the trunk of which had become lodged under the big oak.

With his third step the sole of his work boot slipped off the tree trunk. He took another stumbling step forward, arms flailing, trying to catch his balance. His bad leg came down hard on a submerged branch, and even though it was underwater he could hear the crack as the wood splintered beneath his weight.

A heartbeat later he found himself in water above his waist, his leg pinned by the broken branch. For a moment the shock took his breath away. Fighting back a wave of pain, Nate reached out and snagged Matty's arm, pulling him close. "Don't move," he said. He dragged off his coat before it became waterlogged and wrapped it around the shivering little boy. "My leg is stuck. I'm going to try and get loose so we can get out of the water, okay?"

Matty nodded, huddled in the folds of the heavy coat, his legs stretched out stiff in front of him, one hand fastened like a leech around Nate's wrist. His eyes were filled with tears and his little nose was as red as a cherry.

Nate took a couple of deep breaths and pushed the focus of pain to the back of his mind so that he could think. He tried to move his weakened left leg but it was pinned tight. He didn't have a cell phone, and even if he had there was no guarantee he could get a signal down here. He didn't even have a pocketknife to try and cut away his boot. He was trapped until help arrived, and so was Matty.

"We're going to have to stay here for the time being, buddy." The cold water was seeping into his work boots and his leg was getting numb, but the numbness didn't lessen the pain of damaged tendons and ligaments strained beyond endurance.

"I don't want to stay here," Matty said, the tears spilling over onto his cold cheeks as he began to sob. "I want my mommy."

"She'll be here soon," Nate assured him. He reached out and wiped away the icy tears with the pad of his thumb. "Real soon." He clenched his teeth so that they didn't chatter. He glanced at his watch. A few minutes after two.

The trouble was he knew his sisters. They shopped till they dropped, pregnant or not. It would be at least a couple of hours, maybe longer before Sarah got home. And then there was no guarantee she would think to look for them down in the ravine once she figured out they were missing.

He just hoped he had the energy left to yell loud enough to catch her attention when she did show up. He'd sure picked a hell of a day to get himself into a fix like this one. Harm was halfway to North Carolina with Dan, his mom was busy with insurance work. Neither his dad nor Brandon were likely to drop by.

"I want my mommy," Matty repeated, sobbing helplessly. "I don't like it here. I want to go back home and watch Clifford." Nate wrapped his arms tight around the small sturdy body and held him close, concentrating only on surviving until help came, trying not to think about the pain in his leg and the deadly cold that was creeping up his chest to squeeze the breath from his lungs and eventually slow his heart to a stop.

CHAPTER TWELVE

"I CAN'T BELIEVE IT. I've got everything on my list, Joann's been fed and watered, Sarah's got a new coat and boots for Matty, and it's only one-thirty. Ladies, I think this Day-After-Thanksgiving-Fowler-Sister-Shopping-Spree can be proclaimed a success." Tessa crossed her arms over her massive stomach and leaned back in her chair, a tired, but pleased smile spreading across her face.

"I still have to find *The Incredibles* Xbox games for the boys," Joann said, spooning up the last bites of a mammoth hot fudge sundae, the restaurant's signature dessert. Sarah and Tessa had ordered the eatery's famous homemade chicken noodle soup accompanied by hot rolls and honey, and a house salad. Joann had had the soup and salad, too, plus a side of garlic mashed potatoes. "And don't be too smug. We haven't found a single thing for Dad. And Granddad Harm is giving me fits like he does every year. 'I don't need anything. I've got stuff I haven't taken out of the box from two years ago,'" she mimicked, in a passable imitation of Harm's gravelly voice.

"That's the truth," Tessa sighed. "Other than my usual sack full of sugar-free chocolate bars from the boys he is extremely hard to buy for. And Mom and Dad aren't far behind." Sarah was sorry to hear this. She'd been hoping for inspiration on what she could give the older family members.

"I think I'll get Dad one of those two-million-candle-power lanterns we saw at Kmart," Joann said, licking the last of the hot fudge sauce off her spoon. "He can stand on the porch and shine it along the dock on stormy nights to check the pontoon and the Ski-Doo without having to go out in the rain."

"With one of those he could signal in the space shuttle for a landing," Tessa said, looking as if she wished she'd thought of the idea herself.

"I know. That's what guys love in their gadgets. Overkill." Joann laid down her spoon. "I can't eat another bite."

Tessa caught Sarah's eye and giggled. Joann shot her a quelling look, folding her napkin and placing it by her empty dish. "What next?" she asked as the waitress set the bill tray beside her left hand.

"Let me get that." Sarah reached out for the check. She wanted to do something to repay Nate's sisters for their kindness in inviting her on their outing.

"No way," Joann said plucking the bill from Sarah's fingers. "My treat."

"This could go on all day," Tessa said, digging in the giant woven tote she carried in lieu of a purse. She pulled out a naked Barbie, its red hair standing up as if it had been electrified, a packet of tissues and her checkbook before she found her wallet.

"Why don't we divide it by three, and then Tessa and I will add the tip since Joann drove," Sarah suggested, a little surprised at herself for taking the initiative. The Fowler sisters exchanged one of their glances and then nodded agreement.

"Good idea," Tessa pronounced. "It's twenty-six dollars and change."

"Here's my share." Joann handed over a ten. "And here's a couple more for the tip. I had the dessert," she reminded Sarah.

"And the mashed potatoes," Tessa added as she stowed the Barbie back in her tote.

Sarah anted up and Tessa added her own bill to the tray. "Okay, anyone having buyer's remorse on anything they bought this morning? Wrong size, wrong color? Just plain can't-imagine-why-I-thought-who-ever-I-bought-it-for-would-want-it?" She looked at Joann and then Sarah. "Last chance for returns or exchanges." Sarah and Joann shook their heads. "Then let's go home."

They left the crowded restaurant in a flurry of

packages, coattails and trailing scarves, and made their way through the mall. While they walked, the sisters debated what were the best gifts for their parents and grandfather, and two elderly great-aunts on their father's side whom Sarah had never met. She listened with only half her attention. She was concentrating on what she might give Nate for Christmas, a special gift from her and Matty, yet one that wasn't too personal. She didn't want to overstep the emotional boundaries they'd established in their unorthodox marriage.

They pulled out of the busy parking lot and headed west toward Cottonwood Lake. Tessa seemed to run out of steam the moment her bottom touched the car seat. She leaned her head against the window and appeared to be asleep. Joann turned up the volume on an FM station that was already playing Christmas carols nonstop and began to hum along. The windshield wipers swiped away at the gently falling snow leaving Sarah, cocooned in the warmth of her new down-filled coat, alone with her thoughts.

She leaned her head against the high seat back and stared out of the tinted window into the chilly afternoon. It was all so complicated. She was beginning to feel so at home with Nate's family. With him. Almost as if they were still in love with each other. But they weren't in love. She was grateful to him and he felt responsible for her, that was all. She had to remember that. She couldn't stay in a loveless marriage and neither could Nate. Sooner or later it would destroy them both. She and Matty would have to go, and quickly, before it was too late. There was no other solution. She turned her head to the glass and watched the snow fall.

"We're here," Joann announced. "Tessa, wake up." She reached over and gave her sister a little shake. "Time to unload this stuff." She turned in the seat and stared at Sarah over the console that divided the two captains' chairs. "We always dump all the kids' presents in Nate's workshop," she explained.

"They never mess with things in Nate's workshop," Tessa added with a yawn, as she stretched her arms over her head.

"Ty is past the Santa stage but he's the snoopiest kid I've ever seen," Joann admitted. "Jack still believes in Santa, at least I hope he does, so I make sure it's all out of the house and that way his big brother isn't tempted to peek at the gifts and spill the beans." She put her hand on her stomach and gave a little chuckle. "I thought this would be our last Santa Christmas. Now I'll get to do it again next year."

"And the year after that and the year after that for quite a few Christmases to come," Tessa chimed in. She opened the van door and stepped out into snow that came over her shoe tops. "Wow, we got our own little lake effect going on in Riley's Cove. There's at least an inch more snow here than there was in Adrian."

"You can play in the snow later. Grab your stuff. If we don't dawdle too long we can take over getting supper on the table and give Mom a break. Sarah, are you and Nate coming to eat with us?" Joann asked as she hauled open the door to Nate's workshop, turning sideways to make it through the narrow opening with her half-dozen sacks of Christmas gifts. "Obligatory leftover turkey and dressing supper, ya know. Hey, Nate, anyone here?" she hollered. "Deserted. He and Matty are probably at the trailer." She opened the big metal cupboard that stood behind the futon, a fifties-era storage unit, too heavy and too utilitarian to have any other role, and began piling bags inside. "Here, give me yours, Tessa. Sarah, anything you need to keep out of sight?"

"No. I only got the gloves and boots today. I couldn't decide whether to get Matty the toy dump truck or the workbench and tool set."

Tessa pointed to the hammer and chunk of wood sitting in the middle of the green indoor-outdoor carpet. "My infallible gifting instinct says go with the workbench and tool set."

"Mom can get him the dump truck," Joann seconded.

"She doesn't have to do that."

"Of course she doesn't," Tessa said, making *tch-ing* sounds with her tongue. "She wants to. It's Christmas and Matty's part of the family now." The words gave Sarah a warm feeling that had nothing to do with her new coat, but even though she was pleased to have her son accepted as one of the Fowler clan, she couldn't shake the anxious feeling that had plagued her on the ride home.

"I wonder where Nate and Matty are?" There were tools and parts scattered across the workbench, the lights were on, the Four was out from under its dust sheet, the radio playing the local station. It wasn't like Nate to leave things so untidy.

"Would you do us a favor, Sarah, and tell him we dumped the goodies on him again this year? We really should get going to pick up the kids."

"Of course. What time do you want us for supper? Can I bring anything?"

"No!" Both sisters chorused in unison and then laughed.

"No," Joann repeated. "There's more leftovers than we can eat in two meals. Five-thirty should be fine. That way Brandon won't be tempted to wolf down his food and dash off to party with his friends right away."

Tessa shut the padlock on the storage cupboard and they went outside. They walked toward the van, Sarah now the only one still carrying packages. "Do you need help with those?" Joann asked.

"No, they're not heavy, only bulky." Sarah turned her head toward the trailer. She could have sworn she heard Nate call her name, but no one was in sight.

Tessa opened the passenger door and prepared to heave herself onto the seat of the van. She stopped with one foot on the frame. "Did you hear something?" she asked.

The afternoon was quiet, the wind still, the snow falling silently all around them. "I swear I heard someone call Sarah's name."

"So did I," she whispered. No one spoke. A crow cawed as it winged along the lakeshore, a squirrel scolded from high in the oak by the barn, and then it came again, faint, echoing, but clearly her name.

"It's Nate," Sarah said, dropping her packages as she spun around, trying to figure out where the call had come from.

Joann closed the driver's door very quietly and came to stand beside Sarah. "It sounds like he's at the bottom of a well."

"The creek," Sarah said, with awful certainly. Her heart beat hard and fast, and her breath misted around her head. There was no reason for Nate to be down there on a day like this unless something had happened to her son.

"Nate. Matty." She had never run in snow before and the rubber soles of her shoes slipped and slithered, almost sending her tumbling more than once.

She could hear Joann and Tessa behind her, but she didn't wait for them to catch up. She skidded to a halt at the top of the steps and looked in horror at the scene below.

Nate was in the water up to his waist, coatless, his hair and shoulders frosted with snow. Matty was sitting on the tree trunk that blocked the creek's flow, wrapped in Nate's coat, cradled in his arms, his head resting on Nate's chest as he sheltered him from the weather and the water that lapped just inches from where he sat.

Sarah hurtled down the steps, both hands on the wooden railing to keep herself from falling headlong on the slippery risers. "Nate? What happened?" Matty had opened his eyes at the sound of her voice and started crying and calling for her, arms out held.

Nate tightened his grip, soothing the little boy. "I told you she'd come," he mumbled and Sarah's heart lurched in renewed fear. His words were slurred, his movements sluggish and uncoordinated.

"Shh, Matty, it's all right, honey. Momma's here." She couldn't reach Matty from the bank. She would have to go into the water as Nate had.

"Stay there," he ordered, reading her thoughts, shaking off the terrible lethargy that seemed to have gripped him.

"Nate? Sarah? Oh my God—" Joann and Tessa were at the top of the steps.

"Call 9-1-1," Sarah commanded. Nate wasn't the only one who knew how to give orders. "Hurry."

"My cell's in the van." Joann was already halfway down the steps. She stopped and turned back. "Don't you dare come down here, Tessa," she warned.

"I'm pregnant, not incapacitated. I can help."

"Someone has to make the call and show the EMTs where we are. Call from Nate's trailer. It's closer. And bring blankets back with you. As many as you can carry."

Tessa didn't waste time arguing—she was out of sight before Joann finished speaking.

"I'm coming out to get Matty," Sarah said as Joann came to stand beside her.

Nate shook his head, slowly, deliberately, as though even that small movement took great effort. "Don't try it. There's too much debris in the water. My leg's trapped under a branch."

"Can we lift it, Nate?" Joann stared into the dark, slow-moving water. Sarah looked, too, but she couldn't see anything, and that, of course, was the problem.

"Momma!" Matty was sobbing so hard he hic-cupped. "I want my mommy."

"I'm coming in." She shrugged out of her coat. She didn't want to be hampered by its weight if she slipped under the water.

"Sarah, don't."

She ignored Nate's hoarse directive. "If I get him you can try to free yourself."

"I've been trying," he said, but he didn't argue further.

Joann took Sarah's coat and hung it over the railing. She held out her hand. "Hold on to me as long as you can." Sarah nodded, shivering already in the damp cold. Joann's fingers closed tightly around her wrist.

"The EMS is on its way." Tessa's voice floated down from above. "I'll stay here to guide them down."

"Call Mom, Tessa," Joann yelled back as she braced herself to take some of Sarah's weight. "She'll see the unit turn up Nate's road and have a coronary."

"I already did," Tessa informed her sister. "Dad and Brandon were both there, thank the Lord. They're on their way." She saw what Sarah was doing. "Be careful," she urged.

Sarah stepped off the bank with Tessa's warning ringing in her ears and gasped as the freezing water soaked her from toe to thigh. "My God," she breathed, unable to hold back the exclamation. How had Nate stood the cold for so long?

She took one careful step, then another, letting her leg slide along the sunken tree trunk that had trapped Nate. Joann released her grip and Sarah felt momentarily bereft. She took another step and held out her arms. "Matty, come to Momma."

With robotic motions Nate moved her son farther along the oak trunk until he was within her reach. Matty grabbed onto her hand, whimpering. "I'm cold."

"I know, sweetie. Just a moment more." She gathered him in her arms, coat and all, holding him tight.

She turned carefully and retraced her steps. Her legs felt numb and heavy, the muddy bottom of the creek sucking at her waterlogged shoes. Joann was on her knees on the creek bank waiting to take Matty from her. She handed him over, ignoring his renewed sobs. She couldn't leave Nate alone in the water. "Give me Nate's coat," she said. Joann had anticipated her words and already had Matty wrapped in one of the heavy woven throws Tessa had tossed down the steps.

Sarah took a moment to don her own coat and then, clutching Nate's heavy canvas jacket to her chest, took a deep breath and started back. He was watching her, his hands splayed on the oak trunk to keep his weight off his bad leg. "You can't get me out of here. It'll take two men at least. Go on back."

She wrapped the coat around his shoulders and turned the collar up to protect his ears. The tips were white and blotchy. She reached out to touch him, unable to help herself. "Oh, Nate. I think you've got frostbite." She was shivering already.

"So will you, and worse, if you don't get out of the water."

"I'm staying," she said with finality, hoping the effect wasn't spoiled by how hard her teeth were chattering.

"Never could get you to follow orders," he said. He dropped his head, breathing heavily as though the words took all the strength he had.

"How long have you been in the water?"

"An hour, maybe a little more."

This wasn't Houston or Detroit. The emergency techs were volunteers, the unit housed in the township building halfway around the lake. She didn't know how long it would take them to get there. She moved as close as she dared, wishing she could find a way to share her body heat without getting caught up in the tangle of half-rotten branches herself. She could hear car doors slamming, Tessa calling for Tom and Brandon to hurry, and almost sobbed with relief. "They're here. Your dad and Brandon. They'll get you free."

CHAPTER THIRTEEN

NATE SAT UP and swung his legs over the side of the high, narrow hospital bed. At least they'd given him the bottom half of a set of washed-out scrubs to wear under the damned open-up-the-back hospital gown. It was after 10:00 p.m. and he was still in the curtained cubicle in the emergency room of the small county hospital. They hadn't formally admitted him or moved him into a regular room, so he figured he had a good chance of getting his way if he stuck to his guns.

"I'm not spending the night here and that's final." He'd had all the poking and prodding, warm compresses, hot liquids and IVs and CAT scans he could face. His head spun and the ache in his knee and ankle made him sick to his stomach, but he ignored the pain and closed his eyes until the vertigo went away. He opened them to find his second cousin, Courtney Riley Jenkins, scowling back at him from beneath strongly marked brows, while Sarah watched anxiously from just inside the doorway.

"I swear you're the most stubborn man on the face of the earth," Courtney grumbled, switching her attention to a computer screen attached to a swivel arm on the wall. The device was positioned so he couldn't read what it said, and that aggravated him, too. He put on his best first sergeant face and frowned back at her. It didn't faze Courtney a bit. It never had. She was two years older than he was, but they'd spent most of their childhood hanging out together at Harm's place. She was divorced, twice, the mother of three, a nurse practitioner with a group of doctors in the medical building adjacent to the hospital. Most of the Fowler clan were her patients.

Everyone except him. She probably wondered why, but had never asked. And he wasn't about to tell her in front of Sarah.

It was just his bad luck she was on call in the ER when he came in.

"My temp's normal, my reflexes are good. The frostbite on my ears is minimal. There's no reason to keep me here." She still didn't look convinced. She punched the stylus onto the computer screen with more force than absolutely necessary. He dropped the topkick routine and tried a little charm. "I promise I'll go straight to bed the minute I get home." She opened her mouth to object. "And stay there," he added, trying to form a smile through cracked lips.

He felt like hell, but he'd spent too many nights in hospitals to ever do so voluntarily again.

"You were in fifty-degree water up to your waist for over an hour in below-freezing temperatures," she pointed out in the same tone of voice she probably used with her Alzheimer's patients. "For someone a little older, a little thinner, a little more out of shape, it could have been fatal."

"I'll see that he does as he's told." Sarah spoke with quiet assurance from her spot by the door. Nate refused to meet her eyes. Half of what was wrong with him wasn't a case of mild hypothermia and exposure. It was remorse. Plain old-fashioned guilt at how badly he'd failed her, how rotten a father he'd been the first chance he got to act the part. Maybe that was why God had made him sterile? Because He knew he wasn't any good at raising a child?

"I'm still inclined to keep him overnight," Courtney hedged.

He was at the end of his patience, and about at the end of his strength. If he didn't get this settled soon he would probably keel over where he sat and be stuck here for days. "Sarah, you don't have to stand around here listening to us argue. You should be with Matty."

"Your mother took him home with her," she replied quietly.

"You're sure he's all right? No hypothermia? No frostbite?"

"Just cold and scared. And hungry. Your mother promised him chicken nuggets and apple sauce."

He closed his eyes briefly. Now he was keeping her away from her son, who was probably still half scared out of his mind. The hits just kept on coming.

"I checked him out myself," Courtney chimed in, eyeing Nate closely. "He's upset about losing his football, but getting a close look at a fire truck helped make up for it. I recommend you put a fence across that stairway down to the creek, though."

"First thing in the morning."

Courtney rolled her eyes. "I should have had you restrained and sedated when I got the chance." She took his wrist in a firm grip and checked his pulse against her watch. She stuck the tabs of her stethoscope in her ears and listened to his heart and lungs for about the sixth time. "Okay, I give up. You can go home. But I want you in my office first thing in the morning for a follow-up. I'll have the CAT scan of your leg by then and if you need to see the surgeons at the VA hospital for any reason we can call and set up an appointment. Otherwise, I'll stick to my original diagnosis of a bad bruise and strained ligaments. Stay off it for the next couple of days and it should be okay."

"As okay as it's ever going to be, you mean."

"That, too."

"Deal," he said. "Now, where are my clothes?"

She pointed to a sodden heap of clothing in a nearby sink. "Sorry, we don't have a laundry service here."

"My mother-in-law sent dry clothes and shoes for Nate." Sarah came forward to stand at the foot of his bed. He stayed where he was, hands splayed on the mattress, staring down at his bare feet, his left ankle already black and blue, he noticed. He studied Sarah from the corner of his eye. Her face was pale, her eyes shadowed, and tiny fatigue lines were etched at the corners of her mouth.

"It's a good thing your mother's organized, otherwise you'd be going home in what you're wearing now. And heaven knows where I'd find a pair of slippers to fit those size twelve clodhoppers of yours."

"Courtney has no regard for other people's feelings. She rubbed my nose in the dirt regularly when we were kids," Nate said.

"I had three older brothers," she explained, entering data on the computer screen with a stylus as she talked. "Nate was the first boy I could beat up on. I was six and he was four. It was heady stuff."

"She did it regularly until the winter I grew three inches. That summer I got grounded for a week for putting her in a headlock at the family reunion," Nate responded on cue. Courtney was testing his mental acuity with the seemingly inane conversation and they both knew it.

"You got taller, not smarter. You don't beat up on a girl in front of all the aunts and uncles." She flicked off the computer screen and pushed it back against the wall. She turned to Sarah again. "We never met when you and Nate were first married, did we? I was living in California then. It's a little belated, but welcome to the family." Like the rest of the Rileys and Fowlers, Courtney probably knew the reasons behind their sudden remarriage, but her words were genuinely friendly.

"Thank you." Sarah held out the dry clothes. "I guess he's ready for these."

"I guess. Come with me, Sarah. I'll show you where to sign him out." She pointed her finger at him. "Straight to bed and then my office tomorrow. Ten o'clock. Sharp. Understood?"

"Yes, ma'am."

"I'll send the orderly to help you dress."

He opened his mouth to protest then thought better of it. "Thanks," he mumbled instead, watching as she pulled the curtain, shutting him in the cubicle with no better company than his thoughts.

"I HOPED YOU'D BE ASLEEP by now." Nate's voice was little more than a stirring of the darkness.

She was sitting on the side of Matty's bed watching him sleep, trying to banish the terrifying image of him and Nate in the water that plagued her thoughts, waking or sleeping. She had heard Nate get up and start down the hall and she'd held her breath, afraid he might have a dizzy spell, lose his balance and fall, but he didn't. Now his shadow crowded out the faint glow from the nightlight in the bathroom that filtered out into the hallway. "I got up to check on Matty," she said.

"Is he okay?" He took a limping step into the bedroom, holding on to the door frame for support. The hallway was too narrow to navigate on crutches, he'd told her when she'd offered to fetch the pair that she'd noticed weeks earlier propped in the corner of the closet. He leaned down to touch the tips of his fingers to Matty's forehead. "Does he have a fever?"

"No," she whispered. "He's fine," she repeated patiently. "Not a scratch on him."

Nate put one arm on the headboard, letting it take most of his weight. He reached down and pulled the covers close around Matty's shoulders. "It's cold in here. I'll turn the thermostat up on the furnace."

It wasn't cold in the bedroom. It was almost too warm. Was Nate having some kind of delayed reaction to the hypothermia? Was he chilled because he had a fever? How fast did pneumonia develop? She tried to recall the list of symptoms that Courtney Jenkins had said to be on the lookout for and came up blank.

She stood up and hurried around the end of the set

of twin beds Nate had bought to replace his queen-size mattress while she was in the hospital. So that you can rest comfortably, he'd said, and Matty can have his own bed. She'd offered to buy them from him when she had a place of her own, and he'd shrugged and said they'd talk about it later. They never did speak of it again, but she'd added their approximate cost to the growing column of figures in her notebook.

"It's nice and warm in here." She reached up to touch his forehead the way he'd touched Matty's. "Are you chilled?"

He wrapped his strong fingers around her wrist before she could touch him. "I'm colder than hell," he said with a self-mocking smile that even in the near darkness she could see never reached his eyes. "I don't think I'll thaw out completely until spring." She could feel the fine tremors running through his fingers and her heart constricted with worry. She had promised Courtney she would watch over him, and she was obviously doing a terrible job.

"Do you want some more warm milk? Coffee? Cocoa?" Warm liquids, but no alcohol. She remembered that from the instructions for treating hypothermia. Warm compresses to the head and feet…and groin area. Her stomach muscles tightened. And sharing body heat. No. That wasn't a good image to conjure in her mind, either. Nate was watching her, his eyes shadowed by the night and the barriers he kept up against her so much of the time. "You should go back to bed," she whispered, suddenly very aware that she was wearing only a thin nightgown and her panties. "Matty's fine. He'll sleep until morning."

"You're sure?" he asked stubbornly, turning his head to watch the sleeping child. His jaw tightened, "He won't have nightmares or anything like that?"

"He might," she conceded. "But I'll be here for him if he does."

"God, I'm sorry, Sarah."

"There's nothing to be sorry for," she said a little too loudly, too forcefully. Matty frowned in his sleep and turned over, drawing his knees up so that his little bottom stuck up in the air. He pulled his blankie close and snuggled his cheek into the pillow.

"I should have locked the back door. I shouldn't have dozed off." He was shivering now.

She wasn't going to convince him he wasn't to blame for Matty's willfulness while he was in this mood. Nate took responsibility for everything. It was part of his nature, a trait reinforced many times over by his years in the military. "Go back to bed. Everything will be better after you've gotten some sleep." She led the way down the hall and he followed her, limping heavily. He lowered himself onto the mattress with a stifled groan. "Does your leg hurt?"

"It aches like the devil."

"Did you take the pain pills Courtney sent home with you?"

"I just did."

"Then they should start to work soon. Lie down," she urged once more.

Absently he began to rub his thigh. "I keep hearing him crying."

She couldn't bear the despair in his voice any longer. She dropped to her knees beside the bed. "It was an accident, Nate. Children wander outside all the time. Don't apologize for living in a place where you don't have to keep the doors locked. You can't blame yourself because Matty snuck away from you. If anything, it's my fault for not warning him strongly enough about staying away from the water. But I didn't want to make him afraid—"

"Okay, I get your point. It was nobody's fault."

"Exactly."

"Doesn't absolve me of responsibility."

Courtney had been right. He was the most stubborn man on the face of the earth, at least when it came to beating up on himself. She changed tactics. "Matty wasn't crying when I found you. What did you do to keep him quiet?" she asked.

He stared at her a moment, his brow furrowed as he considered her question. "I told him stories about the war," he said at last.

"The war?" It wasn't what she expected to hear.

"Not war stories," he said, the faintest of smiles lifting the corner of his mouth. "Stories about Iraq, about a camel named Ahmed and a little boy, Usman, who rode him across the desert to bring shoes and toys and candy back to the other children in his village."

"And where did Usman get the shoes and toys and candy from?" she asked, rocking back on her heels. She answered her own question before he could reply. "I think I can guess. From a brave and handsome U. S. Army sergeant."

"Not quite." His smile got a little wider and her heart beat a little faster. "That would be too lame. It was G.I. Joe and his commando squad. It was a pretty good story if I do say so myself. Especially considering I wasn't at the top of my form."

"Oh, Nate." Tears welled up in her eyes and she did nothing to stop them. "I can never repay you for what you did today."

His smile faded. "How many times do I have to tell you, you don't owe me anything." He reached out and wiped the tears from her cheeks with the pads of his thumbs. "Not money. Not gratitude. Nothing. Don't cry, Sarah. I never want to see you cry."

She thought of all the times she'd cried during their first marriage. She had never considered how profoundly her tears had affected him then, how inadequate he felt to deal with her low self-esteem and fear of rejection that haunted her every action. Oh, how she wished she could go back and change the past. But she couldn't, she could only try and make amends now. "I'm not crying because I'm sad, Nate. These are tears of happiness. You love him, don't you? You love my son."

"With all my heart," he said simply, his eyes locked on hers, searching her face. "And I still—"

"Shh—" She put her fingers to his lips.

"I won't say it," he promised. He pulled her close against him and let out a long, slow breath. "Don't leave me, Sarah," he whispered against her throat.

"Nate, please—"

"Just for now. Just for tonight. Stay with me."

How could she leave him? He had saved her son's life. He needed her, and deep inside, beneath the scar tissue of old hurts and the nagging anxiety of new uncertainties, she needed him. He pulled her down beside him and she didn't resist. "I'll stay, but only for a little while." He caressed her cheeks, her eyelids, the curve of her ear. He threaded his fingers through her hair and held her still for a mind-emptying kiss.

"Oh, God, it's been so long," he murmured against her throat and then he fell silent. Nate pulled her nightgown over her head and dropped it on the floor. She hesitated for a long moment, struggling with doubts. Then she took a deep breath and shut down her thinking, rational self and just let herself feel. She was a woman who had been too long without a man. She needed this as much as he did and her body wasn't to be denied.

She helped him shrug out of his T-shirt so that they could lie heart to heart, skin to skin. He moved his mouth to her throat, her collarbone, the upper swell of her breast. He took one swollen nipple gently between his teeth and she felt a bolt of passion from her heart to her womb. His beard was rough and exciting against the softness of her breast. She sucked in her breath on a moan as he circled her nipple with the tip of his tongue.

She reached down and tugged his sweats down over his lean hips, wrapped her hand around him and remembered how big he was, how he had filled her almost to the point of discomfort. A tiny measure of reality intruded. He felt her stiffen, a slight withdrawal she couldn't help.

"What's wrong, Sarah?" he asked, raising himself on one elbow to look down at her. His eyes were dark pools of night but she could see the concern on his face, hear it in his voice.

"It's not going to be the same," she whispered. "We're not the same…I'm not the same. I…I've had a child." And another husband, she thought, but couldn't bring herself to say it.

"And I have a leg full of metal pins and scars. Does that make any difference to you?"

"Of course not," she said indignantly.

He smiled. "Tonight let's not think about what we can't change about the past, or can't foresee in the future." He pushed her panties off her hips and kicked off his sweats, sighing a little with relief when she reached down and tugged them off his bad leg.

"Oh, Nate," Even in the pale shaft of moonlight that was the only source of light in the small room she could see the surgical scars that crisscrossed his leg from thigh to ankle. She reached down to draw her fingertips over the silvery tracing. "I'm so sorry."

"Don't be," he said. He reached down and covered her hand with his. He lifted it, settled it on his erection, then groaned again, this time with pleasure, not pain. "I'd much rather you touched me here."

He had never talked to her that way before, never told her what he wanted, what she should do for him. And the insecure, inexperienced girl she'd been had never asked. Now she did and reveled in the low dark growl of his response.

She slid her leg along the hard contours of his abdomen, straddled him, let him lift her carefully astride him. Her breasts skimmed his chest, her legs bracketed the powerful muscles of his thighs. She lowered her mouth to his and opened her lips, opened the very center of herself to the thrust of his tongue and his body, let him fill her, over and over, until they were both breathless and spent.

Nate wrapped her close in his arms and tucked her head beneath his chin. Her breathing was slow and even. She was asleep and so he allowed himself to whisper aloud what was in his heart, "You're both mine now, you and Matty, and I'll never let you go again."

"NATE, WAKE UP!"

The high-pitched, little-boy voice in his ear jerked Nate awake. "What?"

"Hi." Matthew had his chin in his hands, elbows propped on the mattress, his face inches from Nate's. His hair was standing up in spikes all over his head and he had a streak of cinnamon sugar on his chin and a chocolate milk ring around his mouth. He was wide-awake and smiling, looking none the worse for yesterday's ordeal. "Are you awake?"

"I think so." The light in the room was leaden, the way his head felt. He was stiff in every muscle and his leg ached with a dull, steady pain. He tried to sit up and realized he was naked under the sheet. All the memories of the night before came rushing back. He pushed himself up against the headboard.

"He's awake, Mom," Matthew hollered over his shoulder.

Nate winced. "What time is it?"

"Breakfast time." Matty darted out of the bedroom into the hallway.

Nate eyed his sweats, neatly folded at the foot of the bed—Sarah must have done that—and left them where they were, figuring he'd never get them on before Matty returned.

He was right. Ten seconds later Matty poked his head around the door frame and looked in the room again. "He's still awake," he announced.

Sarah's head materialized above Matty's. "Good morning," she said.

"Good morning." He took his cue from her slightly formal tone.

She ruffled Matty's hair. "You can go watch TV if you want. I think SpongeBob is on."

"Okay." He pattered off down the hall to the living room.

"I fixed breakfast. Oatmeal and toast. But I can scramble you a couple eggs if that sounds better," she said. "And if your leg's bothering you I'll bring you a tray." She didn't move into the tiny room but stayed in the doorway. She was fully dressed in jeans and a sweatshirt, her hair pulled up at the sides and fastened by a clip that looked like tortoiseshell, or whatever you called it, a jumble of browns and golds that matched the silky streaks of color in her hair.

"Don't bother. I'll come to the table. I lost track of my watch. What time is it?"

"Ten-thirty."

"Oh, hell. I missed my appointment with Courtney."

"I called and told her you'd taken the painkillers and were sound asleep and I didn't want to wake you. I hope you don't mind."

"Of course I don't mind. You're my wife."

She made no response to that. "Courtney agreed sleep was the best thing for you. The CAT scan was okay, by the way. Just bruises and a mild sprain as she suspected. She reminded you to stay off it, and to call her if you had any questions or problems. The skin on your ears will probably start peeling in a couple days, but there shouldn't be any lasting damage. Do they hurt?"

"Some," he admitted. The tips of his ears felt like a bad sunburn, but nothing worse. "Thanks for making the call. How long have you been up?"

"A while. I…I didn't want Matty to find me in your bed."

Nate could hear the little boy out in the living room, singing along with the SpongeBob theme song. The kid had a good voice for a three-year-old. "We need to talk about last night, don't we."

She moved a few steps into the room and sat on the edge of the bed, as far as she could get from him in the confined space. "Last night shouldn't have happened, Nate."

He ran his hand through his hair. He knew where she was going with this. "Maybe it shouldn't have happened. But it did." He chose his words carefully. "And it wasn't just sex, Sarah. Or even some kind of emotional release. It was more. You have to admit that much."

She looked down at her hands. "I'm not denying it. Physically we were always in sync. But that wasn't enough to save our marriage four years ago. It would be a mistake to think it would be any more successful today."

"It won't happen again," he said, anticipating her next argument.

She gave him a little half smile. "You sound very sure of yourself."

"I am," he said. "You have my word."

"Well, I'm not as certain of my willpower as you are," she replied with a rueful grin. "Perhaps I should rethink Matty and I staying here until after the holidays. It's a very small trailer, after all."

Nate took heart. She was all but admitting she was falling in love with him again. Wasn't she? "I thought you didn't run away from your problems anymore," he challenged.

Her chin came up. "I don't."

"Then stay. We'll take it one step at a time. See if we can't find some other things that are still good between us and go from there."

CHAPTER FOURTEEN

"DO YOU MIND if I borrow space at the workbench?" Sarah asked, pulling the barn door closed behind her to keep out the cold.

"Be my guest," Nate said. He was crouched beside the Four tightening a bolt. "I've seen that lamp before," he said with a hint of laughter in his voice. "My mother con you into rewiring it for her?"

"Shame on you. She didn't con me. And it doesn't need to be rewired, just a new plug. Your dad's been too busy to fix it so I volunteered," Sarah said.

"It's as old as I am." The lamp's base was an ivory-colored ceramic ginger jar, a classic design that had never really gone out of style.

"Older, actually. Your mom said it was a wedding gift. But it's in good shape and it would cost a pretty penny to replace. Especially since it's one of a pair. And I don't mind doing it, really. It's lonely in the trailer with Matty away for the day."

"*Mi* tools *es su* tools," Nate said with a grin. She found herself grinning back.

They had spent the remainder of the long holiday weekend pretending their lovemaking in the dark hours of Saturday morning had never occurred. They'd eaten Thanksgiving leftovers and delivery pizza, watched Disney movies and played Chutes and Ladders with Matty while Nate kept his bad leg elevated and one eye on the football games on TV. He had been as good as his word, never crowding her, or even allowing himself to brush against her if he could help it, not an easy feat in the close confines of the trailer. She had appreciated the effort, but one small corner of her heart had wished he would sweep aside all her carefully reasoned arguments and take her into his bed again.

It had been a relief to both of them when Nate insisted his leg could stand the strain of working on the Indian and he'd hobbled off to the workshop. Now, a week after the accident, the bike was ready to be delivered to its owner in the posh Detroit suburb of Birmingham, and they were getting pretty good at ignoring the sexual tension that still radiated between them.

"I'm going to fetch Matty from Tessa's when I finish this," Sarah said as she inspected the wire leading from the lamp base to the broken plug. No nicks or cuts so she decided it didn't need to be replaced. "Is there anything we need from the carry out? I'll pick it up on the way back."

"How about a twelve-pack of beer. Granddad's

back in town. That means he'll be stopping over now and then for a cold one, and there's none in the fridge." Nate pointed over his shoulder with the wrench to the ancient, electricity-gobbling refrigerator emblazoned with motorcycle and racing decals at the end of the workbench.

"You know if you replaced that dinosaur with a new, energy-efficient model it would pay for itself in a couple of years. That thing probably uses enough electricity to light up half of Riley's Cove."

"I thought I'd wait until you go back to work at HomeContractors," he said.

"Ah, my employees' discount." She cut off the broken plug and tossed it in the oil drum Nate used as a trash can.

"Exactly."

"I think that could be arranged." She connected the stripped wires to the new plug and tightened the connection. She slipped the prongs into one of the receptacles on the workbench and turned the switch.

"Good as new," Nate said from near her shoulder. She jumped a little. She hadn't noticed him leave the bike and move to stand beside her. "Sorry, I didn't mean to startle you."

"That's okay. I...my mind was on something else."

"What?" he asked quietly. He was leaning against the workbench, wiping his hands on a faded red cloth.

"My period started today," she said bluntly, not looking at his face but replacing the wire strippers and the screwdriver in their respective drawers. "So you…we…don't have to worry that I might be pregnant from…from what happened between us last week."

"That's probably a relief to you," he said. There was no emotion in his voice, no relief. No regret. He wasn't the kind of man who wore his heart on his sleeve, or spoke easily of his deepest feelings, so she shouldn't have expected anything else. She promised herself she would always keep that aspect of his makeup in mind when they were discussing emotional matters. After all, these were dangerous waters. This was the subject that had destroyed their first marriage.

"It would have made an already complicated situation untenable," she said, but despite the warning she'd just given herself, she couldn't stop herself from searching his face for some clue to his feelings. They were learning to speak of what was closest to their hearts but it was slow going.

"You're right about the complications. Thanks for telling me," he said, and walked back to the bike.

"I would have loved the baby no matter the circumstances, you know that don't you, Nate?"

He turned and met her gaze but his gray eyes remained shadowed. "I don't doubt that for a minute."

"But it really is for the best. It really is," she repeated, and she wondered if it was to convince herself as much as him. She wound the lamp cord around the base and changed the subject. "I'd like to work on a couple more picture frames this evening if you don't mind." One afternoon while he was resting his leg Nate had gone through the snapshots of Matty and the other kids that she had taken over the fall and suggested that she frame some of them for his parents and sisters as Christmas gifts. She'd loved the idea and decided to try her hand at making the frames herself to personalize them even more.

"You're welcome out here anytime."

"Except when you're painting," she said, daring to tease him a little.

"Sawdust and paint sprayers do not mix well," he agreed. He switched on the headlamp of the Indian. The beam shone brightly against the wall. He gave the chrome lamp one last flick of the cloth. "She's done," he said. "I'll crate her up tomorrow and deliver her Wednesday."

"And then you'll start work on the Harley?" Frank Heller had arrived back in Riley's Cove the day before with the motorcycle in tow.

"Or Frank will," he said, running his hand lightly across the back fender.

Sarah set the lamp back on the workbench and

stuck her hands in the pockets of her coat as she turned to face him. "What does that mean?"

"It means I might have a new job come the first of the year."

"Are you going back into the Army?" Was that his way of bringing their marriage of convenience to an end, by applying to return to active duty? Would he ask her to go with him? Would she say yes?

"No. My leg's too beat-up to get back on active duty. I know, I tried."

"Then what kind of job is it?"

"One with benefits and a 401k plan."

"A desk job?"

"Well, yes and no," he said with a rueful smile. "It will be a desk job for a year or so. While we're setting up the program." She saw a glint of laughter in his eyes and knew he was teasing her by giving out his news in bits and pieces, but she didn't mind playing along—for a little while anyway.

"What kind of program are you talking about?"

"Last summer I taught a gun safety course at the community college when the regular instructor had bypass surgery. I enjoyed it but it was a one-time deal, or so I thought."

"Now they want you back?"

"Not exactly. But the head of their criminal justice program, my boss, has been hired by a small, private college near Hillsdale. They want him to set up a Reserve Officer Training Corps program. He needs an experienced NCO. He called today and asked me if I wanted to apply for the job."

"Oh, Nate. You'd be good at it."

"I think I might be. At least I'd like to give it a try. It's the closest I'll get to being back in uniform again. There will be a lot of face-to-face with the kids, and not an improvised explosive device in sight, other than about one hundred eighteen- and nineteen-year-olds handling live ammunition on the firing range." His mouth curved into a grin. "What do you think?"

All thoughts of their teasing give-and-take fled from her mind. "In the old days you would have made the decision and then told me about it." She couldn't stop herself; the words just came out.

His mouth tightened for a moment, then softened again. "You're right, I probably would have. But that was then and this is now."

"What about the restorations? The Harley?"

He looked down at the Indian. "I can still work on the bikes in my spare time, and in the summer. It's great being self-employed but I need to think of the future." This time she had no trouble reading his thoughts. He was including her and Matty in that plan.

But is that what she wanted, too? She couldn't stay in a loveless relationship. Sooner or later it would destroy them both. Did Nate love her? Did he want them to have a real marriage? A partnership? Did she have the courage to find out? No, she realized, as her heart thumped against her chest, not yet. But she could make the first move. She took a deep breath. "I think you should pursue it," she said.

"I was hoping you'd say that." He took a step toward her and suddenly Sarah was ready to throw all the rules about boundaries out the window. They weren't the same people they'd been four or five years ago, when things went sour. Nate was right. That was then. This was now, and the tantalizing image of a future together beckoned once more.

"It's colder than a polar bear's backside out there today." The door opened and Harm came in stomping his boots to free them of snow. "Got any beer?"

"Welcome back." Reluctantly, Nate stepped away from Sarah as he turned to greet his grandfather. "Sorry, I'm out of beer. Sarah's going to pick up a twelve-pack at the store later." He wished the old man had timed his arrival a little better. If he'd had ten more minutes alone with Sarah they might have started saying what was really in their hearts instead of tap-dancing around what was to become of their sham marriage.

"That's okay. It's a little early in the day. Been up since four-thirty though, so it seems later."

"How was your trip back?" Her tone was breezy, but there were spots of color on her cheeks and Nate could see her breasts rise and fall as she tried to get her breath back under control.

"Traffic wasn't bad but we drove hard to get back here before the snow."

"The weather man's predicting three to five inches tonight. Do you think it will last until Christmas?"

Harm shook his head wisely. "That's more'n two weeks away. Snow never lasts too long this early in the winter."

Sarah looked disappointed. Nate sometimes thought she was even more excited by the prospect of a white Christmas than the children were. "Oh well, maybe it will snow again before the holiday."

"Likely will."

The door burst open again and Becca raced into the workshop, mittens flapping from the sleeves of her coat where they were attached by little metal clips, a furry purple hat covering her cinnamon curls. Matty was right behind her bundled up against the cold in a new snowsuit. He'd reluctantly given up wearing his Michigan ball cap in favor of a toque that covered his ears and tied under his chin, but still sported a big block M on the front.

"Hello, Becca Boo. Hello, Matty."

"When did you get home, Grandpa?"

"A couple of hours ago. Got up in the middle of the night to get here ahead of the storm."

"I missed you." Becca threw herself into her great-grandfather's arms. Matty was more reserved but he smiled, too, and came forward for a hug when Harm held out his arms to him.

"Hi, Granddad," Tessa said, following the children into the workshop and closing the door on the winter wonderland scene outside. "It's coming down by the shovelful out there."

"Tessa, you should have called me. I was planning to pick Matty and Becca up and deliver them to pageant practice," Sarah said. The three-year-olds were participating in the Christmas Eve Nativity play at the church Nate's family had attended for four generations.

"You can still do that if you want. I need to stop by the post office and mail a package. It will go more quickly if I don't have quite as much help," she said, pointing at the two little ones.

"I'd be happy to chauffeur."

"Wonderful. I'll bring Matty home after practice, so don't worry about coming back to get him."

"I appreciate that."

"Good, that's settled." Tessa hitched her big bag higher on her shoulder. "I'd better get going. There might be a line at the post office and it won't do for the pageant director to be late. I'll stop by later and hear how your trip was, Granddad. I hope you have pictures of Gar in his dress blues."

"Course I do. Sarah's not the only one who can take pictures, ya know."

"Can't wait to see them." Tessa gave them all a wave and waddled out the door.

"Tell us about your trip, Harm." Sarah said, reaching out to straighten Matty's hat, which had slid sideways, leaving one ear exposed to the cold.

"It was good. The Marines have changed a lot of things since I was a grunt. But a lot's stayed the same. Dan's boy's been accepted for Recon training. He found out the day before we left Lejeune."

Sarah shook her head in wonder. "I remember Gar being a skinny kid with braces following Brandon around the summer we were married. Now he's a Marine. You must be very proud."

"Proud and scared stiff—same as I was when Nate went overseas. Being in Recon means he'll be shipping out sooner rather than later."

Becca was dancing from one foot to the other. "Did you bring me a present?" she demanded.

"I might have," Harm admitted.

"Goody! I like presents."

"Me, too," Matty chorused hopefully. Harm rubbed his finger along the edge of his nose. "I don't know. I hear you were kind of a bad boy while I was gone."

"I won't go outside alone again," Matty said solemnly. He'd been lectured over the last week, gently but firmly by the entire family, and even one or two of the neighbors, just as if he was one of their own. Nate had a feeling the lesson had been learned, but he wasn't letting down his guard. A smart, inquisitive kid like Matty was bound to get into more scrapes as he got older.

"In that case I think there might be a little something for you, too, down at my place. Erika picked them out," he told Sarah. "She got the shopping gene like all the rest of the Riley women."

"Yeah! A present. Can we have them now?"

"You need to go potty and wash your hands and face before we go to pageant practice," Sarah reminded her son gently. "If we go down to Granddad Harm's house first we'll be late."

"They'll still be there next time you come by," Harm added.

"We want our presents now," Becca demanded. Two lower lips emerged in identical pouts.

Nate thought it was time he stepped in. "It's getting close to Christmas, remember? Santa Claus will be checking to see if you're being naughty or nice."

"Nice! Nice!" they chorused.

"We'll visit Granddad Harm soon," Sarah promised. "Now let's get going."

"Take your time," Nate cautioned, even though he'd promised himself not to lecture her on her lack of winter driving skills. "And watch out for slick spots."

"Yes, sir." She ushered the children out into the snow.

Harm waited until the door closed behind Sarah and the children. "Your mother says it was a near thing for you and Matty."

"It wouldn't have been a big deal if I hadn't gotten hung up on that submerged branch." Nate didn't embellish his statement. He figured his mother had already filled his granddad in on the details. He swung his good leg over the frame of the Four and settled onto the leather seat. He was going to miss the bike when it was gone. But he was excited about the prospect of the ROTC job, too. The bikes had filled a real void in his life over the last year but it was time to move on.

"Still, it was a good thing you were there."

"He walked out of the trailer on my watch," Nate said, wiping away a smudge on the chrome handlebars with a shop rag. He had put the incident into some kind of perspective over the intervening days, but it still bothered him.

"I see you put a snow fence up along the creek bank. That should remind him not to go there. Might be a good idea to do a little kid-proofing around my place before spring, too, since it seems like Matty and his mother are going to be sticking around."

Nate narrowed his eyes and stared at the old man. "How do you know that?"

"I've seen the way she looks at you when she thinks no one is watching," Harm said, shuffling over to the old futon and lowering himself stiffly onto the seat. "My eyesight isn't that bad." Nate hoped his granddad was right. He sure hadn't been able to detect her softening toward him—except for a few minutes ago. He took heart from the observation.

"She hasn't made up her mind what she wants to do, yet," he replied carefully.

"Have you asked her to stay? And I don't mean in this brother-sister type arrangement you've got going on."

"Not in so many words."

"Don't wait too long, boy. Sarah's a woman who knows her own mind these days. But that don't make her a mind reader. Don't be so stiff-necked and close-mouthed she gets tired of waiting on you to step up to the mark and walks out of your life again. This time for good."

CHAPTER FIFTEEN

"COME ON, NATE. I want to get our Christmas tree." Matty was stomping around Tessa's kitchen floor in his boots, hopping from one linoleum square to the next as though playing hopscotch. Thankfully the boots were soft-soled or Nate wouldn't have been able to hear half of what Tessa was saying.

"Matty, quiet steps," Sarah admonished, putting her finger to her lips.

"I'm squishing monsters." The little boy kept on jumping, landing flat-footed with considerable force.

"Stealth mode, soldier," Nate said, in his best imitation of Matty's talking G.I. Joe figure.

"Okay." Matty began tiptoeing around the big room, imaginary weapons held at the ready.

"I'm going to have to remember that one," Sarah said with a grin. She smiled more often these days, Nate had begun to notice. He hoped that was a sign that she was more comfortable with him, with their situation. He'd sure done his damnedest to give her all the time and space she needed, but the strain was beginning to take its toll on his nerves and his libido. "Here, let me do that," Sarah said, slipping to her knees to wrestle with the stubborn zipper of Becca's coat.

"Thanks." Tessa put her hand at the small of her back as she straightened up, red-faced. She was wearing a red maternity smock adorned with reindeers and candy canes over a pair of black stretch pants. She'd told Sarah she'd ordered the smock from Omar the Tentmaker, and Sarah had laughed, but to Nate's inexperienced eye his sister looked enormous. "Remember, Nate, seven feet is okay for the tree, but no taller or Keith will start sawing away at the base because Grandma Fowler's angel light won't fit on top without banging the ceiling. And you know he never gets the cut right. Our tree always tilts one way or another," she explained to Sarah. She clapped her hand over her mouth. "Don't tell Daddy I said that," she cautioned Becca. "It will hurt his feelings."

"Okay," Becca said, pretending to lock her lips and throw away the key.

"Do this," Sarah said, spreading out her fingers. Becca obeyed and Sarah slid her gloves onto her hands. The splayed fingers thing was another one of those "mother tricks," like never actually saying "no" to a three-year-old if you could help it, that Nate was beginning to pick up on.

Tessa settled Becca's furry purple hat on her head

and snuggled it down over her ears. "There, you're ready to pick out the perfect Christmas tree."

"Let's go," Matty urged. "I'm getting hot."

"We'll have her back in an hour or two," Nate promised his sister.

"You're sure it won't be too much trouble with both of them tagging along?"

"She's no problem at all. We're happy to have her."

"Good, then I'm going to park myself on the couch and take a nap. I didn't get a wink of sleep last night."

"Did you see the way Tessa kept rubbing the small of her back," Sarah said under her breath as they followed the children out to the truck. "That's where my labor pains started with Matty."

"She's not due for another two weeks."

"The baby's dropped and on her last visit she said the obstetrician told her she could go any time. I think you'll have a brand-new nephew by Christmas."

"Then it's a good thing Keith will be home tomorrow night. He can keep Becca occupied so that Tessa can get some rest." He knew having a baby was a natural thing, but it still made him nervous as hell to think about the mechanics of it. They strapped the kids into their seats and climbed into the truck.

"Where are we going to get the tree?" Sarah asked as they drove down Main Street past the display of trees the Rotary Club had set up outside the town hall, and turned to head out of town at the corner of Church Street, where the sign in front of the First United Methodist church announced the time and date for the Christmas Eve pageant.

"I thought we could cut our own," he replied. "That way it'll be fresh enough to leave up until New Year's Day. There's a tree farm a few miles out of town."

"I've never been to a tree farm."

"It may not be Christmas-card-perfect weather, but we'll do the 'pick it out, chop it down and drag it back' thing anyway."

"I wish the snow hadn't melted." It was a gray, blustery day, warm for December, with low banks of rain-heavy clouds being pushed along by strong, gusty winds.

"We can turn around and go back," Nate said, watching the little ones' reaction to his suggestion in the rearview mirror. "Wait for tomorrow? Granddad Harm says it's going to snow tonight. His knees hurt and his arthritis is usually more accurate than the Weather Channel. What do you say, kids? Should we wait another day or two?"

"Nooo! We want to get our trees now," Becca insisted.

"Me, too." Matty agreed.

"What about you?" he asked, turning to Sarah.

"Oh, no, you don't," she insisted with a sparkle of mischief in her brown eyes. "I've never had a real Christmas tree in my life. I don't have any more patience than the children. If you turn this truck around I'll wrestle the steering wheel away from you and Becca and Matty can push you out onto the side of the road."

"That sounds like mutiny to me."

"Darned right. Are you with me, kids?"

"Yeah!" Matty pumped his fist in the air. Becca didn't look as certain about a mutiny.

"Please, Unca' Nate. Let's go get the tree."

"Your wish is my command," he said, but he was looking at Sarah when he said it, not at Becca.

A few minutes later they turned down a farm lane and pulled up outside a turn-of-the-century white clapboard house with green shutters and gingerbread trim on the wrap-around porch. Behind a three-car garage was a huge, red, hip-roofed barn, easily twice the size of Nate's. A real, working barn full of livestock and farm machinery.

A heavyset, balding man of about Tom and Arlene's age came out of the house to greet them. He was Neil Compton, the owner of the farm, and a friend of Nate's dad's from high school. "Nate, good to see you. Come to get a tree?"

"Two of them," Nate said.

"Need an axe?"

"Got a chain saw in the back." Tradition was a good thing, but a well-sharpened chain saw was even better.

"You can drive down the lane to the lot."

"What's the price this year?"

"Twenty-five dollars for the ones over six foot. Fifteen for the smaller trees. That suit you?"

"Sounds fair to me," Nate said, pulling out his wallet. "We need one of each."

"Forty dollars then. That includes sales tax. The small trees have a red tag on them. The big ones are yellow. Makes it easier to judge the height and saves having to cut off the end when you get it home. Do you need any help?"

"I think we can handle it."

"Then I'll get back to my chores."

Nate heard cows mooing from inside the barn. So did the children. "Are those 'Away in the Manger' cows?" Becca asked.

His niece was an enthusiastic singer and drilled Matty relentlessly on the words to her beloved carol whenever they were together. *I think the kid's got a future in the Corp; she's a born DI,* he had confided to Sarah as they eavesdropped on them one day.

"Perhaps Mr. Compton won't mind us looking in on his cows when we're done cutting down our trees. What do you think, Nate?" Sarah asked.

"I think that could be arranged."

"AHHH. I DON'T LIKE COWS! They're too big." Becca buried her face in Nate's shoulder and began to wail.

"They smell. Let's go." Matty was practically crawling up Sarah's pant leg to avoid the gaze of one of the curious Holsteins who had poked her head over the top of her stall to check out the strange humans.

"They won't hurt you," she soothed. The tree cutting had gone off like clockwork, except for Becca being momentarily frightened by the noise of the chain saw starting up, but Sarah was beginning to think this side trip through the cow barn wasn't such a good idea.

"They're huge," she whispered, resting one hand on Nate's sleeve.

"You tend to forget how big a cow is until you're standing right next to one," he agreed.

"What should we do?" Sarah asked. "If we leave now they'll both be traumatized for life." She was only half joking.

Nate's brow furrowed for a moment. "Hey, do you want to sing 'Away in a Manger'? I bet the cows would like that."

Becca stopped crying and peeked out from under the brim of her hat. "You think so?"

"I read somewhere that cows like music," Nate said, treating the matter as a serious scientific discussion.

"Everyone likes Christmas music." Sarah smiled

her gratitude. Nate was a natural with kids. She wished he would recognize that about himself. Maybe he would now that he was seriously considering the ROTC position, although she supposed she was stretching the comparison between college freshmen and three-year-olds. "I bet Mr. Compton's cows do, too."

Becca stared uncertainly at the six box stalls on either side of them, each containing an interested bovine resident.

Nate reached out to pet a big head. "Don't let it bite you," Matty warned, still safely behind Sarah's leg.

"It won't bite me. But she might like your hat," Nate said, eyeing Becca's furry purple chapeau. "It looks good enough to eat."

Becca's blue eyes grew big as saucers and she clamped her hand on her head. "My hat isn't good to eat. Even for a cow." She leaned a little closer but didn't loosen her stranglehold on Nate's neck. "Purple fur is pretty, cow. But it doesn't taste good."

Matty ventured out from behind Sarah and began tugging on Nate's pant leg. "I want to pet it."

"You do?"

He glanced over at Sarah, who nodded and held out her arms to take Becca from Nate, so he could lift Matty up. "Are you sure she's not too heavy?" he asked, looking anxious.

"I'm sure."

Becca wrapped her arms around Sarah's neck and gave her a hug. "You smell good. Way gooder than the cows," the little girl pronounced.

Sarah laughed. "Thank you. I think."

Nate hoisted Matty up, and angled himself between the cow and the little boy. "Just in case Old Bessie gets too curious," he said over the top of Matty's head.

Matty held out one little hand and patted the cow between the ears. "She's soft," he giggled, looking at Nate with shining eyes. "But she still smells bad."

"I'll pet her," Becca decided, stretching out her left hand, waving it in excitement. "I'm not afraid anymore." Sarah moved slightly closer to the stall and Becca reached out with the tip of one finger to touch the cow's velvety black ear. "She really is soft, just like my hat. Can we sing to them?"

Sarah glanced at Nate and he shrugged. "I don't know why not."

"Away in a manger," Becca warbled, and Matty followed suit. When they started to falter halfway through the verse, Sarah joined in and helped them finish. The cows listened attentively, shaking their great heads as though to say "thank you" when the impromptu concert ended.

"They liked it, Becca," Matty said, his eyes full of wonder. "Just like my dad said."

Sarah heard Nate's quick intake of breath. She felt

her own catch in her throat. Matty had announced he wanted Nate for his daddy at Thanksgiving, but hadn't mentioned it again. Sarah had thought he'd forgotten about it, but she had been mistaken.

"What should I do?" Nate whispered.

"Nothing," she replied. "It…it was probably just a slip of the tongue. I…I'll explain to him if it happens again." She felt her heart constrict at the disappointment that flickered briefly behind his gray eyes.

"Let's go now," Becca announced imperiously. "I want to tell Momma I petted a huge cow."

Sarah patted her cheek, surprised to find her hand was trembling. "You're a brave girl."

"Yes," Becca said, beaming. "I am."

"Ready to go home, Matty?"

They walked out into the fading glory of a winter sunset, all terra-cotta and smokey-blue with streaks of silver along the horizon and the crisp tang in the air that presaged the snow that would come in the night.

"Goodbye, cow." Becca waved over Sarah's shoulder.

"Piggyback ride, Nate!" Matty giggled.

Nate swung her son up and settled him on his broad shoulders. "You're right," he said, in the carefully neutral tone he used to hide his deeper feelings. "It probably was just a slip of the tongue. But I wouldn't mind a bit if he did it again."

"BOY, AM I GLAD you guys are back." Tessa said, meeting them at the door.

Nate was wrestling the big balsam they'd cut for her out of the back of the pickup as Sarah came up the steps with Matty and Becca by the hands. Tessa had changed her clothes, Sarah noticed. "What's wrong?" Her sister-in-law was pale, her great blue eyes shadowed with pain.

"I'm in labor. The contractions started early this afternoon but I just thought they were gas, or something I ate, you know how it is. But then my *water* broke about half an hour ago. Mom always said the second one comes faster than the first. Now I believe her."

"How far apart are they?" Sarah asked, shooing the children on into the kitchen so that Nate, unaware of what was happening, could get the big tree through the door.

"They started at five minutes but the last couple have only been three minutes apart. I tried to call Mom and Dad but they aren't home. I keep getting Joann's voice mail—she must be in a meeting or something. I was just about ready to drive myself to the hospital when you pulled up." Tessa appeared composed, but beneath the calm exterior Sarah sensed the apprehension of a woman facing labor without the father of her child at her side. It was a situation she had endured herself, and would do anything she could to spare Nate's sister. "I really didn't want this to happen until Keith got home."

"Didn't want what to happen?" Nate asked innocently, peering at them through the branches of the tree he'd set upright on the throw rug by the door. He tipped the tree sideways and stared hard at Tessa. "Are you all right?"

"I'm in labor." She sat down abruptly as another contraction began. Her hand curled into a fist as she waited it out. Sarah glanced at the clock on the microwave. She could see Tessa struggle to stay focused and hide her pain from Becca and Matty.

"Mommy, are you all right?"

"Whew, that was a doozy," she said, letting out a breath. "I'm fine, Becca Boo. But it's time for the baby to be born. I have to go to the hospital to get him, remember?"

"I don't want you to go." Becca was crying now and Matty was tearing up in sympathy. "Call them, tell them just to bring the baby here."

Tessa hugged her daughter close. "I can't do that. The baby is in my tummy. I need the doctor and nurses to help get him out."

Nate stood rooted to the kitchen floor. He could lead men into battle and disarm a makeshift bomb with a pair of tweezers and a nail clipper, but he obviously didn't know what to do with a woman about to give birth. Time wasn't going to stand still, nor would the baby wait on them to get organized, so Sarah began issuing orders.

"Nate, go put the tree in the stand. We can't just prop it up against the wall and leave it there. While you do that I'll get Tessa's suitcase and then you drive her to the hospital. I'll stay here and try and track down your parents and Joann, feed the children and keep them occupied." No one moved. Sarah felt like stamping her foot like Matty did when he wasn't getting the attention he wanted. "Nate. Now!"

"Yes, ma'am." He sketched a salute and hustled the tree into the adjoining family room.

"The stand's already set up in front of the window," Tessa called after him. As the contraction eased she relaxed against the back of the chair, smoothing Becca's hair and rocking her back and forth in her arms. "My suitcase is in the hall closet," she said, hauling herself up with Becca still holding tight to her arm. She pried the little girl's fingers loose one by one. "Becca, go with Sarah. You can watch videos with Matty and have pizza. It won't be very long until we have our new baby and then you can come to the hospital and see him."

Five minutes later, Sarah watched as Nate bundled Tessa into his truck and came around the hood to get into the driver's seat. "Drive carefully," she said.

"I'll drive carefully but very, very fast." He

looked grim and determined. "I guess you figured out by now I don't know nothing about birthin' no babies."

Sarah laughed and stood on tiptoe to give him a brief kiss. "You'll do fine."

"Stay close to the phone," he said.

"I will." She watched him back out of the driveway with exaggerated care and then roar off into the deepening twilight. Sarah wished she could be there for Tessa, but it was more important to her sister-in-law that Becca be well cared for. A hospital waiting room was no place for two overtired, overexcited pre-schoolers. She turned back to see two teary-eyed little ones looking lost and forlorn at the kitchen door. She smiled. "Who wants to help me fix pizza?"

"I do," Matty said, jumping up and down, waving both arms in the air.

Becca wasn't as easily distracted. "I want my Mommy," she sniffed.

Sarah went down on one knee and wrapped her in a hug. "I have an idea."

"What?" Little arms stole around her neck and held on tight.

"I saw that your mom has everything ready to decorate the tree. After supper we'll all pitch in and make it beautiful for her when she gets home from the hospital with your new brother."

"We have an angel for the top." Becca's sobs had dwindled away to a sniffle now and then.

"I know. She's very old, I understand."

"She's older than my grandma."

"Oh, my, as old as that? But she's still pretty, I bet. I can't wait to see her."

Becca let out a long, heartfelt sigh. "I'm glad our baby is getting born but I still want it to be a girl."

CHAPTER SIXTEEN

"SARAH, WAKE UP." Nate leaned over the back of the couch and traced his fingertip along Sarah's cheek. Startled, her eyes flew open and she stared at him for a moment. He withdrew his hand and curled his fingers into a fist on the back of the couch. It was the first time in close to three weeks he'd given in to the almost constant urge to touch her.

"I must have fallen asleep," she said, sitting up. She lifted her hand to her cheek. "What time is it?"

"A little after midnight."

"Did Tessa have the baby? Are they both all right?"

"Both of them are fine."

"What time was he born? How much did he weigh?" She was whispering but he could hear the excitement building in her voice, watch it chase the drowsiness from her big brown eyes.

"Seven pounds, thirteen ounces. Twenty inches long. Blue eyes. A little bit of blond hair. And her name is Ashlyn Elizabeth." He saw her stiffen slightly and her eyes flew upward to meet his amused gaze.

"Ashlyn? Elizabeth? But I thought—"

"We all did, but it seems the ultrasound was wrong. It happens more often than you think, the midwife said. Looks like Becca is getting her Christmas wish a few days early. Her baby brother is a girl." He looked across the room at the nest of quilts and blankets containing two sleeping three-year-olds beside the tree whose bottom third was decorated with an overabundance of ornaments. "When did the kids give up and go to sleep?"

"About nine. It was a long day for them."

"For all of us. God, the chairs in that waiting room were designed for little people." He sat down beside Sarah and propped both feet on the coffee table, massaging his aching knee. "Umm, it smells good in here. I'm glad we picked the balsams."

"Exactly how I always dreamed a live Christmas tree should smell," Sarah agreed. He laid his arm across the back of the couch and Sarah turned to face him, tucking her stocking-clad feet up under her. "Everything went okay?" she asked, returning to the subject that was most important to her. They had decided he wouldn't call from the hospital with updates because it would only keep the kids agitated, so Sarah was in the dark about the details of his sister's labor.

"I guess." He gave a mock shudder. "I'd rather clear a mine field with a butter knife than go through that again. How do you women manage it?"

"The reward is worth the pain," she said with a Madonna smile that twisted his heart. "Details," she prompted, once more.

"Mom and Dad and Joann showed up about an hour after we got to the hospital. Until then it was just me and Tessa." He flexed his hand, wincing. "She has a grip like a pro wrestler."

"What about Keith?" Sarah rested her arm alongside his and propped her chin on her hand. The silkiness of her hair against his skin made him shiver.

"He was out of cell phone range until about eight o'clock, but when we got through to him the nurses were great about rigging up a speaker phone so he and Joann could talk her through the really tough spots. He's getting a few hours sleep while they load his truck, then he's heading home. He should be here late in the morning."

"Were you with Tessa the whole time?"

"No, ma'am."

"Your mother was with her," she said with a knowing smile.

"Actually, she and Dad stayed with me in the waiting room."

"That surprises me. I thought Arlene would take charge of everything."

"Mom talks a tough game but she's a real softie when it comes to one of us being in pain. She just couldn't take it."

"I'll have to remember that next time she's doing her General Patton impression," she said, still smiling.

"In that case, you didn't hear any of this from me."

"I won't blow your cover. Ashlyn Elizabeth— such a pretty name. Who does she look like?"

He frowned. "Why do women always ask that question? She looks like a baby," he said truthfully. "Red and wrinkled and crying."

His observations were obviously inadequate. "Didn't anyone take pictures?" Sarah asked, horrified at the omission.

"Joann took some with one of those disposable cameras from the hospital gift shop. She's getting them developed in the morning."

"It would have been great if someone had had a digital camera," Sarah said wistfully. "Then you could have downloaded them to Tessa's computer right away."

"Wait a minute. My brain's fried. I forgot about the hospital's Web site. The delivery nurses take pictures of all the newborns. You just have to know the baby's surname and date of birth to call it up. Tessa was the only mother in labor so the nurse said she'd have time to scan Ashlyn's picture in tonight. Let's boot up the computer and take a look." He stood up and held out his hand. For a moment he thought she would refuse his help rising from the couch, but after a slight hesitation she let him fold his palm around hers.

He led her across the room to Tessa's computer and typed in the hospital's Web site. A few clicks later the scrunched-up, red-faced image of his niece appeared. She was wrapped in a pink blanket with a tiny pink hat on her wispy blond curls.

"She's beautiful," Sarah whispered.

"I think she looks as if she's disgusted with the entire universe at the moment," he said.

Sarah gave a little laugh. "She probably is. She's been warm and well-fed, and tucked just beneath her momma's heart for nine months. Now all of a sudden it's cold and noisy, and her momma's nowhere to be found. You'd cry too if your world was turned upside down that way. But she's going to be a beauty, just like her sister and mother. I can tell."

"She does have Tessa's stubborn chin and Becca's snub nose," he agreed.

"So beautiful." She reached out to touch the screen as though the little one were really there. Her wedding ring gleamed in the light of the monitor. He couldn't help himself. He reached out and traced the warm gold with the tip of his finger.

He heard Sarah draw in her breath. He turned his head and she was staring at him, her eyes liquid and dark. "Sarah," he said, reaching out to cup the back of her head in his hand. He was tired of waiting, tired of keeping his distance. He wanted her, needed her, and he couldn't keep it to himself any longer. He kissed her, long and slow. She resisted, but only for a moment, then she wrapped her arms around his neck and settled onto his lap.

He had kept his silence all through the short, gray December days since Matty's accident. He had given her space, given her time, but his patience was at an end. He had tried to tell her he had fallen for her all over again the night they had made love, but she had stopped him. Now, in the midnight quiet of his sister's house, he would have his say. "I love you, Sarah. I love your son. I want us to be a family."

She rested her forehead against his and gave out a long sigh, as though a burden had been lifted from her. "Oh, Nate. I love you, too. I don't think I ever stopped loving you but I tried so hard to believe I had, I almost succeeded. Until today. In Mr. Compton's barn when Matty called you Daddy. Then I couldn't pretend any longer."

"I love him almost as much as I love you. I'll be the best father I can be to him."

"I know you will." She leaned back a little so that she could study his face. He held himself very still, letting her look deep into his thoughts and his heart. "There's something I need to ask of you."

"What is that?"

"I…I want Matty to know about David," she whispered. "I owe him that much. You understand, don't you?"

"I consider it an honor to take his place in Matty's life and I'll make sure he's not forgotten."

"Thank you, Nate." She brushed her lips across his, not in passion but in promise, a pledge to a little boy and to themselves, making a real marriage of the *pro forma* ceremony they'd gone through many weeks before.

"Don't leave me ever again," he said, his voice gruff with passion and need. His heart beat hard and fast. She was his again. This time forever.

"I won't leave you. We're different people this time, Nate. We won't make the same mistakes we made in our first marriage. We'll tell each other what's on our minds, and in our hearts." She turned her head to look at the baby's image on the computer screen. "I want to stay here in Riley's Cove with you. Have your children. Grow old with you."

She leaned close and he closed his eyes, lest she see the anguish her words had caused him. He should have known the subject of children would be in her thoughts, especially tonight. What should he say? How should he tell her? "Sarah—"

"Umm?" She was kissing him again and he fisted his hands against her back, fighting to stay focused and not give in to the almost irresistible urge to keep from telling her what he knew he must.

"Nate, why are you kissing my mommy?" Matty asked, sitting up amongst the welter of sleeping bags and pillows in front of the Christmas tree. Becca curled up into a ball at the sound of their voices, but she didn't wake up.

"Oh-oh," Sarah said, slipping off his lap. She was blushing and the sight made him smile despite the heaviness in his heart. She went over to Matty and knelt beside him on the carpet. Nate followed her and used the arm of the couch to lower himself to his knees. "Matty," she said. She took his hand and he curled his fingers around hers. "Nate was kissing me because that's what grown-ups do when they love each other."

"You love him?"

"Yes, I do and Nate loves me."

"And I love you, too, buddy," Nate said, ruffling his hair.

"Are you my dad now?" He looked from Sarah to Nate and back again.

Sarah squeezed Nate's hand, waiting while he swallowed the lump in his throat. "Yes, I am."

Matty considered that. "I'm glad you're my dad," he said at last. "But no more kissing on the lips—it's yucky."

"THEN BECCA woke up and started asking about the baby. By the time we got the two of them settled down again it was hard to bring up the subject of my sterility—the moment had passed."

Before his mother could respond, the phone beside her elbow rang. Again. "Oh, dear. I should have unplugged it." He hadn't taken his mother's nonstop pre-Christmas schedule into account when he walked down the hill to his parents' house.

"Joann, hi. I know, it's great about Nate and Sarah. You want to what? Bell them?" She rolled her eyes and made a twirling motion with her hand, indicating she was trying to cut the conversation short. "What's that? In this weather? Look, I'm swamped at the moment. Can I call you back? Okay. Good. Bye, now." Arlene set the receiver back in the cradle and then unclipped the line from the back. "There. No more interruptions."

"Bell us? What the hell's that?"

"I'm not sure. Some old-fashioned kind of impromptu wedding party. She said something about potluck, champagne, banging pots and pans, and riding you two through town in a wheelbarrow."

Her answer surprised a grunt of laughter out of Nate. He never ceased to be amazed at what his sisters could come up with.

"They're happy for you. We all are." Her smile couldn't quite mask the anxiety underlying her words.

"We probably should have held off telling everybody that we're staying together until after Christmas. Both Joann and Tessa are in full-bore entertainment mode this time of year anyway—even with a brand-new baby on the scene." Nate folded his arms across his chest and stared down at his mug of coffee. "Mom, what should I do?"

"You've been reconciled for almost a week. You're telling me you still haven't spoken to Sarah about any of this?" Arlene lifted her mug and took a swallow of coffee, giving him time to order his thoughts. He had seen the question in his mother's eyes every time she'd looked at him the past week, but there had always been others around and she had held her peace. He didn't blame her for wanting to know what he intended to do. He was thirty-four years old but he was still her firstborn child and she worried about him.

He stared past the miniature Christmas tree sitting on a table in front of the window behind his mother's chair. The big snow from the week before was gone, leaving the grass withered and brown but the five-day forecast predicted more snow for Christmas Eve. He hoped the weather guys were accurate for Sarah and Matty's sake. White Christmases in this part of Michigan were pretty rare.

"I keep looking for the right opening, the right

words. It's hard just to come out with it. What do I say? 'Hey, Sarah. Those babies you said you wanted? Forget them. I'm sterile.'"

"What's wrong with just taking her in your arms and telling her?"

"We're living in a trailer with the second nosiest three-year-old in the universe." Arlene let a smile curl the corner of her mouth. They both knew who was the nosiest.

"You know you have only to ask and your father and I will keep Matty for as long as you need."

"I know."

"Are you afraid of her reaction when you do tell her?"

His mother knew him too well. "She wants more children. She told me so the night Ashlyn was born. It was a disagreement over having children that split us up before."

"Sarah's not the girl she was," his mother reminded him in an uncharacteristically gentle tone. "She's a woman now. She loves you. She'll understand. But if you keep her in the dark much longer she'll begin to blame herself. And when you do finally tell her she'll end up blaming you. It would be a no-win situation. Worse than that, it could ruin the trust you'll need to help keep your marriage strong in the future."

"Hell, don't you think I know that." It kept him awake at night. He hadn't slept more than an hour or two at a stretch since his niece was born, even with Sarah wrapped in his arms. "I called for an appointment with the urologist at the VA."

"Good," Arlene said, looking relieved. "You're taking Sarah with you?"

He shook his head. "I want to have all the information I can first, Mom." He set his mug down on the corner of a filing cabinet with a thump. "Maybe something's changed. I want to know if there's any hope at all."

"Nate, this isn't a war game. It's Sarah's happiness as well as your own you're gambling with here. Don't withhold this from her any longer, please. I remember her calling me after you'd shipped out to Afghanistan. When…when it was too late to save your first marriage. Her heart was breaking. She couldn't understand why you were behaving the way you were. She was hurt and angry and wanting you to suffer in return. Maybe if you hadn't been separated, if you could have looked each other in the eye and spoken what was in your heart…? Now you have that opportunity and you're not taking it." She lifted her hand palm up. "I just don't know. I took your side then. I'll stand with you now, but I believe it wasn't all Sarah's fault that you split up. Fate's brought you back together. She's your wife, once more. Your partner. Nate, take my advice. Tell her soon. Don't bottle everything up inside and make the same mistake again."

CHAPTER SEVENTEEN

"Away in a manger, no crib for his bed." Matty was standing ramrod straight before the altar of the First United Methodist church, wearing an old flannel bathrobe that had been Brandon's and possibly even Nate's—Arlene swore she couldn't remember back that far. His headdress, an authentic Iraqi *shimagh* Nate had sent home to Brandon as a souvenir, was cocked over one ear and required frequent straightening by Becca, the angel by his side in silver halo and white robe, who was in full mother-hen mode. But wardrobe malfunctions and even the distraction of two bunnies and a baby pygmy goat in the manger scene couldn't sidetrack the dozen preschoolers in the chorus from singing their hearts out. Sarah had never heard anything sweeter in her life.

She sat beside Nate in the third pew on the left, his family ranged on both sides. Arlene holding eight-day-old Ashlyn, while Tessa and Joann sat in the first pew to help coach their little charges. It was

Christmas Eve and Sarah felt as if a lifetime of deferred wishes were coming true for her and Matty.

When the candlelight service ended they would walk the few short blocks to Arlene and Tom's and have cookies with hot chocolate for the kids and rum-spiked eggnog for the grown-ups. They would open presents and ooh and ahh over the new baby, declaring that she really was smiling at her grandfather—it wasn't just a gas bubble—and when midnight struck they would wish each other Merry Christmas and she'd go home to tuck her son into bed, put his Santa presents under the tree and fall asleep in her husband's arms.

Becca and Matty's part in the Nativity play came to an end. They marched down the aisle, side by side, Matty's brand-new running shoes gleaming white beneath the frayed hem of his robe, and slid into the pew beside Arlene and Tom. Becca immediately began fussing over her baby sister, who was staring fixedly at the overhead lights as she sucked lustily on her pacifier. Matty leaned past Tom and waved at Sarah and Nate, smiling broadly. He, too, was fascinated by the new baby but hadn't yet summoned the courage to do more than let her curl her tiny fingers around his hand. "She might go pee pee on me like she did Becca if I hold her," he had explained to Sarah and Nate a few days earlier when they took him to Keith and Tessa's to see her for the first time.

Sarah smiled at the recollection but didn't let herself drift off into a daydream again of how Matty would react when she became pregnant with Nate's child. There would be plenty of time for such dreams—tonight was for enjoying in the present.

The older children and teens filed into the sanctuary and took their places in the living Nativity. "There's Erika," Matty told her in a stage whisper as he leaned past Tom once more. "See her, Mom? She's Mary."

Sarah smiled and held her finger to her lips, "Shh."

"Oops. Church voice," Matty whispered back.

The pageant proceeded with solemn dignity until one of the lop-eared rabbits broke away from its shepherd handler and went hopping toward the choir loft, its keeper, stumbling over his robe, hopping along right behind it. He captured his charge just before it disappeared under the organist's bench, causing her to miss a chord or two, and brought it back to his place behind the manger. But having tasted freedom, the bunny began kicking and scratching. The young shepherd tried manfully to ignore the renewed escape attempt but it was obvious to the entire congregation that he was losing the fight.

With admirable aplomb, Erika, breathtakingly pretty in blue and white, took the lifelike doll that was portraying Baby Jesus in her arms. The overexcited bunny was safely deposited in the timothy-hay-filled manger where he remained for the rest of the performance. Almost before Sarah knew it, the carols had all been sung and the benediction pronounced, and they were filing out of the church, the strains of "O Holy Night" following them into the cold.

"It was a lovely service, Pastor," Sarah said sincerely, as she pulled on her gloves just inside the door. The rotund, middle-aged minister had visited her in the hospital, but this was the first time she had been inside the small, old-fashioned brick church.

"I'm glad you enjoyed it, Mrs. Fowler, please come again. You are always welcome in God's house," he said, holding her hand in both his warm ones.

"Thank you, Reverend."

"It's snowing! Yippee!" Ty hollered from the bottom of the church steps as Nate and Sarah stepped outside. "Now Santa can use the reindeer instead of driving his rocket sled."

They descended the last of the concrete steps and stopped beside Arlene and Tessa and the baby. Snow was coming down in thick white flakes. If you looked up you could see them swirling out of the darkened sky in a dizzying dance. Sarah held out her hand and caught one on the tip of her gloved finger. It was so big the delicate tracery of its construction was plain to see. "Look, Matty," she said, but he was already trying to scrape together a hundred thousand of the delicate crystals to make a snowball.

Nate looked at her and grinned. "He's all boy."

"Tessa, you and the baby had better ride with your father and me. He's bringing the car around now."

"Yes, mother," Tessa said with mock docility. She looked at Sarah over the top of the baby's blanket-covered head, and winked. "It's as if I'm not capable of caring for my own child at this stage of her life. Mom'll be like this for the next couple of weeks. She always is until the newness wears off."

"Tessa. He's here," Arlene called over her shoulder.

"I think she's in this hyper-grandma mode to make up for not being a superwoman and staying with me for the actual birth itself, but don't you dare tell her I said so." Tessa walked the few feet to Tom's Buick where Becca—official bearer of the camouflage-patterned diaper bag, purchased when Ashlyn had been expected to be named Keith, Jr.—was already ensconced in the back seat. Tessa deposited her blue-clad baby daughter in her mother's arms before sliding in beside Becca and being whisked away—to get all of three car lengths before stopping to let another vehicle back out of a parking space ahead of them.

"We'll get to Grandma and Grandpa's first even

though we're walking," Jack pronounced, bounding off down the sidewalk to lob a snowball at the corner mailbox. "C'mon, Ty, let's run." Joann, Keith and Gus were still inside the church overseeing the return of animals and borrowed costumes, and checking that no "grass-eaters anonymous donations," as Gus put it, had been left on the altar to scandalize the Christmas morning worshipers.

"Guys, slow down. You'll slip and fall in the snow and get your good pants all muddy, and your mom will tear a strip from your hides and mine," Nate warned the excited youngsters.

Matty was holding each of their hands as they walked, laughing in delight as they lifted him in big swinging steps along the sidewalk. The snow was coming down harder all the time, already covering the seared brown grass and the thin coating of ice that was beginning to build up along the edge of the lake. "We're going to open presents at Grandma Arlene's house, right?"

"Yes."

"Then Santa's bringing me more presents tonight?"

"That's right," Sarah confirmed patiently.

"I'm lucky."

"We're all very lucky and very blessed." Sarah looked over at Nate. He had been quiet all evening. In the hectic week since they'd made their marriage a true union, they'd discussed many things, including the feasibility of starting the barn renovations before spring if Nate got the ROTC job, and whether Matty should go to day care when Sarah returned to work, or stay with the high school friend of Joann's who cared for children in her home. There was also the matter of when she should start her business and how long they might have to wait to get it up and running if she got pregnant right away. The slight shiver down her spine had nothing to do with the cold. When they talked of children, Nate grew silent and withdrawn.

Or was she just imagining things? Was she so enthusiastic, so full of hopes and dreams and plans for their future that she wasn't giving him a chance to contribute to the conversation? That was probably what had happened. She needed to slow down, to listen as much as she talked. After all, they were just finding their way through the ins-and-outs of this communicating business.

"We're here," Matty said, as they turned up the walk to Arlene and Tom's house. "Rudolph, the red-nosed reindeer," he sang, as he caught sight of the animal's mechanical namesake Tom had set up in the yard.

"The kid's got a good voice," Nate said over Matty's head.

"So does Becca. She's a good teacher."

"I'm told my grandmother had a lovely voice. She always sang 'Ave Maria' at the Christmas Eve service. My mother says it's one of her earliest memories, and even Uncle Dan swears he can remember her standing before the altar in a dark blue robe with a big white collar, even though she died when he was a few months younger than Matty."

"Is that why your grandfather wasn't at the service tonight?" Sarah asked, thinking she already knew the answer.

"Yes, it's been a lot of years, but it's still one thing he can't bring himself to do."

"He must have loved her very much."

"So much that he says he never found a woman worthy to take her place."

"She must have been a wonderful person. I'll have to ask your mother to tell me about her some day."

"She'd like that."

"Rudolph with your nose so bright, won't you guide my sleigh tonight?" Matty sang as he skipped along.

"Good voices run in our family." Nate scooped her son, *their son*, into his arms and added his pleasant baritone to Matty's piping treble as they walked through the door of his parents' house. Sarah forgot all the nagging little worries of just moments before and gave herself over to the joy of Christmas.

NATE WONDERED how much longer he would have to keep pretending he was having a good time. He leaned one shoulder against the fireplace and stared at the snapshots of Becca, Joann's boys and Matty that Sarah had taken and framed for his parents' gift from the three of them. A fifth frame, still empty, waited for an enlargement of Ashlyn's picture, and a sixth would be added when Gus and Joann's baby arrived in the summer.

But there would never be a photograph of his child. He turned away from the mantel to see his entire family grouped around the living room, ankle-deep in discarded bows and crumpled wrapping paper. It wasn't the sight of them happy and sated that was the cause of his foul mood, any more than it could be blamed on the noise as his nephews drove their remote control ATVs into the legs of the dining room table. It was the Hallmark-card-worthy sight of his wife holding his infant niece that drowned his Christmas cheer as effectively as if he'd pitched it across the road into the middle of the half-frozen lake.

The look on Sarah's face was angelic. He didn't care if the description sounded hackneyed or clichéd. It was the truth, and it seared his soul to watch her so happy and content. She was a born mother. She may have doubts about her self-worth in other areas, but not in this most important one. How was he going to tell her that she would never hold a child of theirs?

His mother was right. He had to find a way to break the news, and soon. Sarah looked at him from across the room, perhaps sensing his bad mood, and he summoned a smile. She smiled back, but her expression remained thoughtful.

"Nate, come on, how about a hand or two of Texas Hold 'Em to break in the set of poker chips your mother got me," Tom said. "Gus and Keith will join us, won't you, guys?" Nate dragged his eyes away from Sarah and Ashlyn to meet his father's knowing gaze.

"Sure, Dad." He might as well play a few hands of cards. It was obvious that the kids were too wound up to go to sleep anytime soon, and the women had settled in to talk about babies, and discuss what dishes they would bring to Christmas supper the next evening.

"I can't afford to play for more than pennies," Keith grumbled good-naturedly as they seated themselves around the dining room table. "Between the hospital bills and Christmas, I'm tapped out. Especially if I opt out of the long-haul runs for the rest of the winter."

"You made up your mind?" Gus asked, admiring the leather case of poker chips Tom set between them.

"Yeah. Tessa's going to need help with the girls and to tell you the truth I'm tired of being away from home so much. Every time I get back from a run

Becca's learned something new. Gets old, telling her bedtime stories over a half-assed cell connection."

"Hey, no more half-assed cell connections in this family," Tom reminded him. "Your mother-in-law got the best coverage plan money could buy."

Keith grinned a little sheepishly. "You're right." He pulled the brand-new, state-of-the-art cell phone that Tom and Arlene had gotten all of them for Christmas off the clip on his belt. "Picture phone, unlimited, any-time minutes for friends and family—"

"Half a dozen new numbers to add to my speed dial," Gus griped.

Keith ignored him. "Coast-to-coast coverage, no roaming fees—"

"And you will keep them on your persons at all times," Arlene instructed as she passed through the dining room on her way to the kitchen to heat Ashlyn's ten o'clock bottle. "Two emergencies in little more than as many weeks when half of you were impossible to reach, or worse yet, didn't have a cell—" she rolled her eyes in Nate's direction.

Nate pulled his cell off his belt just as his brother-in-law had done. "I'll never leave the house without it again," he promised.

"See that you don't." She sailed off toward the kitchen. "All of you."

"And that was no idle threat." Grinning, Keith

picked up his cards. "It's Christmas, brother-in-law. Couldn't you deal me a better hand than this?"

"TOM, STOP SHINING that spotlight at them, they'll be blinded if they look directly at it." Arlene shook her head. "I give up on that man. He's worse than the children with a new toy."

"It's just what I needed for checking on the boat," Tom defended his gift as he reluctantly shut off the powerful flashlight.

"The boat won't be in the water for five months."

"Okay, then, the ice shanty. Can't have it floating off across the lake, now can we?"

Sarah laughed at their good-natured bickering. "Thanks again to both of you for the cell phones. It was a wonderful idea."

"And so were the photographs of my grandchildren," Arlene said as she followed them out the front door onto the porch. "I'll treasure them all."

"I'm glad you liked them," Sarah replied, sounding pleased. Nate's throat tightened with love and gratitude for his parents. He knew how much it meant to Sarah, and to him, to hear his mother include Matty in the phrase "my grandchildren." A faint echo of their voices came back to him from across the lake. The wind had picked up a little during the evening and the big fat snowflakes that had fallen so softly as they walked home from church had turned to bits of icy shrapnel that stung his cheeks and hands as he carried Matty out to the van.

"Merry Christmas," Sarah called one last time.

"The same to you. We'll eat about six tomorrow, but come over any time you want," Arlene responded from the shelter of the porch. She wrapped her arms beneath her breasts and looked out into the gathering storm. "It's really turned nasty. Will you check and see if your grandfather got home all right?" She'd given Harm a cell phone too, but he was already grumbling the buttons were too tiny and all the new phone numbers confusing to an old man who had enough trouble just figuring out how to get the messages off his answering machine.

Nate waved to let her know he would do as she asked and climbed behind the wheel. He'd come outside earlier, when Tessa and Joann and their families had left, to load presents and start the engine so the van was warm and cozy.

"That was the nicest Christmas Eve I've ever spent," Sarah said, as they headed out along the shore road. "The baby was so good. And Becca's such a proud big sister." She chuckled, a wondering kind of laugh, that was half amused, half wistful. "It's been so long since I held a little one. I'd forgotten how tiny they are, how helpless. Why didn't you hold her when Tessa wanted you to?" she asked quietly. "Gus did." There was no laughter, no teasing lilt in her voice this time.

"Gus needs the practice," he said tightly. "And there were too many others in line ahead of me."

"Will you hold her tomorrow?"

"Sure. Looks like Granddad's home safe and sound," he said, grateful for the chance to change the subject. There were lights on in Harm's cottage. The old man opened the door to let the cat in as they passed and waved. Nate tapped the horn once in reply and kept on going up the hill. The back wheels of the van spun on an icy spot underneath the oak. "Getting slippery. We need to see about trading this van in for one with four-wheel drive if you're going to be commuting to Adrian every day."

"That's probably a good idea."

"I'll carry Matty inside and then come unload the presents." He picked up the still-sleeping child and they walked the short distance to the trailer in silence. Sarah opened the door and he laid the little boy gently on the seat of the recliner. She knelt by the chair to take off his coat and hat. The kid was so wiped out he might have been a rag doll instead of a real boy. His arms flopped, he twisted in the seat until he was curled up in a little ball, and his thumb popped into his mouth with the accuracy of a heat-seeking missile on the tail of a fighter jet.

Sarah laughed softly and threw up her hands. "I'll

let him sleep for a little while. If we're quiet we can put his Santa gifts under the tree without waking him."

They had wrapped his presents, a tool set, a batch of coloring books and crayons, a miniature fishing pole—his idea—and a squishy ball with myriad rubbery arms that looked more like a sea anemone than anything else Nate could think of, the day before and hidden them on the closet shelf.

"I'll make a pot of coffee. Would you like some?"

"Sounds good."

Fifteen minutes later he stood beside the small balsam Sarah and Matty had decorated and watched her move around the kitchen, her hair shining in the subdued light from above the sink, her dark red sweater hugging her breasts, her matching gauzy skirt swirling enticingly around her calves. She was feminine and looked fragile, yet he knew the fragility was deceptive. She was one of the most courageous women he knew, strong and resilient.

"Coffee's ready," she beckoned softly. He took his place at the table and watched as she sat down across from him and wondered how he would ever get over her if she left him again.

"I'm too excited to sleep. Do you want to open our gifts to each other tonight?" He knew that she had gotten him a fishing rod and reel. It was hard to hide something like that in the small space they shared. She had given him a similar rig their first Christmas.

"We can if you want to." He ached to give her the sapphire engagement ring he had secreted among the branches of the little Christmas tree, but even the anticipation of that pleasure was tainted by the information he still kept from her.

"Or we can wait until morning if you want." She wrapped her hands around her coffee mug and stared down at it. He was acting like Scrooge and he was ashamed of himself.

"I'm just so impatient to watch Matty open his Santa gifts. It's the first year he's really been old enough to take it all in." She gave her head a little shake and the tiny gold bells she wore in her ears tinkled very faintly. "I'm so impatient to be pregnant, too. This may sound selfish and shallow but I want a Christmas baby, like Ashlyn."

"It doesn't sound that way to me," he managed. Now it was his turn to fiddle with his coffee mug, to avoid looking directly into her eyes.

"I know I've had my share of miracles already this year. The surgery—" She laid her hand over his. "Finding what we lost again." He couldn't help himself, he turned his hand palm up and folded his fingers around hers. "I've decided I'm going to ask Dr. Jamison to recommend a gynecologist when I see her next week, one that specializes in fertility issues."

He couldn't keep staring at his coffee. "Why do

you need to see a fertility specialist?" he asked, keeping his eyes on hers.

"Just…just in case there might be some problem…with me. The surgery, all the medication—"

"It's only been a little over two months since your surgery. Give yourself time." He nearly choked on the words. *Tell her,* a voice demanded inside his head, or was it his heart? *Tell her you can never give her a child—a brother or sister for Matty. That she'll never experience the joy of cradling her infant to her breast.* His heart began to pound as if he'd just stepped on the trip wire of a mine. It would be the same argument and recriminations and tears they'd experienced four years ago. He was convinced of it. It would drive them apart again. And this time there would be no chance for a happy-ever-after ending. His chest was so tight he couldn't breathe. He pushed away from the table and stood up.

Sarah stood up too and came into his arms. She laid her head against his chest and Nate closed his arms around her, breathing in the soft flowery scent of her shampoo and the slightly heavier citrus aroma of her perfume. "I just want to make sure there's nothing wrong with me, that I can give you strong, healthy children."

"There's nothing wrong with you," he said too quickly, too forcefully. *God, he couldn't do this to her, make her feel as though his inadequacy was somehow her fault.*

She lifted her head and scanned his face. "Maybe not with me, physically. But there is something wrong. I saw it in your face when I was holding the baby."

He could feel the muscles in his jaw tighten. Her eyes widened and he read the stirring of uneasiness in their depths. "It was the baby, wasn't it?" she whispered. "You were upset about me holding the baby." A tiny thread of panic seeped into her words. "Why, Nate? Why were you upset by that? I thought you wanted to have a child together. Soon."

He felt like he was back in Iraq, heading out on patrol, not knowing if or when a bullet or a makeshift bomb would find him, but knowing his only option was to move forward. "We're not using birth control because it won't make any difference." He held her at arm's length, fixing his gaze on her bottom lip so that he didn't have to see the pain and disillusion in her eyes. "The hell of it is I can't make you pregnant no matter what we do. I'm sterile, Sarah. We'll never have a child together."

CHAPTER EIGHTEEN

STERILE. She didn't wrench herself from his arms, but clung to him for support. "Was it because of your injury? An illness?"

"I had an infection, one of those nasty ones you can get in the hospital no matter how hard they try to prevent it. They ran some tests." His lips twisted in a humorless smile. "They decided the infection, as bad as it was, wasn't what caused the condition. I've probably always been sterile. In a nutshell, I'm allergic to my own sperm."

"So you didn't know anything about your condition when we were married before?"

"No." At least he hadn't lied to her then, but now— She thought of all her rosy daydreams of the past week, babies and more babies. Her babies and Nate's. Nausea churned her stomach.

"How long have you known?" She whispered past the constriction in her throat. She wriggled out of his arms, needing space to think, to breathe.

"A little over a year."

"When did you intend to tell me?"

"I've been trying to find the right time." He loosened his grip on her as soon as she moved. She hadn't realized how cold the trailer was until the moment when that vast, frigid distance seemed to open up between them.

"The right place. The right time. You've used those words before." She could feel the sobs building up inside her, feel the same pain she had experienced four years ago, and she knew she couldn't bear that heartache again.

"Sarah, please. The last thing I wanted to do was hurt you."

"I remember you saying that, too. But you did hurt me. You're hurting me now. I thought things had changed this time. That we had changed."

"It has. We have," he said.

"No. It's still you who has to be in control. Who does what he thinks is best for me. How long were you going to let me go on wishing and praying I might be pregnant after every time we made love?"

"Only until I could see the doctor at the VA—" He realized how damningly he'd phrased the words and winced, reaching for her again.

Her despair turned to anger. The anger was easier to bear than the pain she felt for both of them. She held up her hand. "Don't touch me."

Nate did as she asked. The stranger he had suddenly become four years ago had returned. "I'm sorry as hell for not telling you the night Ashlyn was born. It was a mistake. I knew it then, I know it now. But it won't change anything. I can't give you a child. I never will be able to." Matty whimpered in his sleep, disturbed by the anguish in their words even though they were whispering. Nate shot a glance over his shoulder at the sleeping child, raked his hand through his hair. "This damned cracker box is too small for us to be arguing. We'll give Matty nightmares. I'll sleep in my workshop."

"No." She dragged the shreds of her pride around her to keep out the icy coldness that had overtaken both his voice and his bearing. She had heard that tone before, over the miles that separated them physically and emotionally as their first marriage had dissolved around her. "I'm not forcing you out of your home. Matty and I will go." She grabbed her coat and purse out of the closet before he could stop her, then bent to scoop her son into her arms. She shrugged off the restraining hand he wrapped around her arm. "Let me go, Nate." She could be as unyielding as he was. "I need to be by myself. I need to be alone."

"It's midnight on Christmas Eve. It's snowing. Where will you go?" There was no more hardness in his words—only resignation and pain. Pain that matched her own. She almost broke down and gave in to her need to stay and be held in his arms.

"I don't know." She thought of the cell phone Arlene had given her just hours before. "I'll call you when I get there."

NATE WATCHED the taillights of the van disappear along the shore road. Every nerve in his body screamed for him to jump in the truck, chase her down and bring her home. But that might goad her into trying to outrun him, which would be suicidal folly on a night like this. The smart thing, the rational thing, would be to wait for her call, go after her in the morning, give her a chance to come to her senses. He turned up his collar against the sting of snow crystals and shoved his hands in the pockets of his coat.

He'd warned her of black ice and he'd told her about deer, the worst road hazard in this part of the country. Always watch for their eyes along the side of the road, he'd explained—they shine like cats. And remember where there's one, there are usually more.

She had Matty with her; she'd be cautious. But careful or not she still wasn't used to driving on ice and snow.

"To hell with waiting for her to call," he growled under his breath. "If she wants out of the marriage she's going to have to tell me so to my face." He grabbed the keys to the truck and headed down the hill after her. He didn't think she'd go to his mother, or Tessa, but he drove by their houses anyway. Both dark, everyone asleep, waiting for Christmas morning. Who else could she turn to? With the exception of the manager of the HomeContractors store and Dr. Jamison, Sarah didn't know anyone outside Riley's Cove. A scene popped into his mind. Sarah pointing out the shabby motel where she and Matty had stayed when they first came to Michigan. Was that where she was headed? What was it called? He racked his brain for a name. Wild something? Wildflower? Wildwind? Wildwood. That was it, the Wildwood Motel. It was as good a place as any to start looking.

Nate was relieved to see that the gravel trucks had already been out when he turned onto the county highway. The fine stone scattered at crossroads and on curves would increase traction and keep cars from skidding out of control. That was what worried him most, that if Sarah went into a slide and she'd panic and lose control of her van. He should have never allowed her to leave, but short of duct-taping her to a chair he didn't know how he would have stopped her.

The whole scenario was almost a carbon copy of what had happened to them four years ago, except this time he didn't have the false luxury of deeming himself to be in the right. The noble warrior, all-knowing, defender of the woman he loved. Nate snorted at this flowery turn of phrase that came into his mind. This time his inadequacy was the cause of her unhappiness. This time the noble thing to do would be to let her go.

"Yeah, to hell with that, too," he said between clenched teeth. "She's my wife and I'm not going to lose her again without putting up a fight." A flicker of movement at the leading edge of his headlights caught his attention. With a graceful leap the yearling doe landed in the middle of the road. Her hooves hit the wet pavement and went out from under her, sending her sliding across the center line where she scrambled to her feet and bounded into the darkness. Nate slowed, then hit the brakes hard when a buck and two more does followed the yearling onto the road. He swore briefly as the pickup's tires slipped on the ice. He attempted to steer into the skid but two seconds later his headlights were pointing into the woods and his bumper was redesigned to fit the imprint of the trunk of a maple tree.

"Damn," he swore under his breath, moving his arms and legs to make sure everything was working the way it should. He unfastened his seat belt and got out of the truck to check for damage. The airbag hadn't deployed, a good sign, he decided. It was hard to tell for sure but it seemed the damage was confined to a dented bumper and a missing chunk of the front grill, but the back wheels had dropped into a small washout and there was no way he was going anywhere without a tow truck to pull him back onto the road.

Nate patted the pocket of his coat for his new cell phone. Not there. With a groan he remembered leaving it on the counter by the stove, along with the neatly typed list of numbers to be programmed into it. He climbed back into the cab and stared out into the darkness. The only sounds were an occasional metallic ping from the cooling engine, and the tattoo of sleet pellets on the windows. Nate pondered his options. Start walking in below-freezing temperatures down a nearly deserted, icy highway, or wait where he was until some good Samaritan came along to give him a ride into town? "I've really screwed the pooch this time," he said out loud, banging his fist on the steering wheel in disgust. "What I could use right now is a big old sleigh and eight flying reindeer."

SARAH STEERED the minivan into the parking lot of the Wildwood Motel and turned off the engine. She sat for a moment flexing her hands to restore the circulation. She'd been gripping the steering wheel so tightly that her fingers were numb. She'd tried to remember everything Nate had told her about driving country roads at night in bad weather. She'd alternated staring at the pavement in a futile attempt to anticipate slick spots with gazing into the near distance in search of the reflective eyes of whitetail deer. She hadn't seen any deer, except for a dead one by the side of the road. She had hit a couple of icy patches, but she'd kept her head and realized it wasn't a lot different than driving on rain-slicked city pavement, which had given her confidence.

She had been so preoccupied with her driving she hadn't had time to regret the things she'd said to Nate, but now couldn't think of anything else. Especially faced with the drab exterior of the Wildwood Motel. The vacancy sign was brightly lit but she couldn't see anyone behind the reception desk through the office's dirty window. "We're here," she whispered, to herself as much as to Matty, who was strapped into his booster seat behind her.

"Where's our house?" Matty asked, rubbing his eyes, bewildered to wake up and find himself in his car seat rather than his bed.

Sarah turned to look at him. "We're only going to stay here for a little while. Just until Mommy figures out what to do." What was she going to do? She was so tired and so confused. How had things gone so badly for her and Nate in such a short time? Sterile? Her Nate—the most virile man she had ever known? How could it be? And when she should have stood by him, assured him she loved him no matter the circumstances, she had run away. It was just the way their marriage had played out four years ago.

She knew her thoughts would circle around those questions over and over, paralyze her with indecision, if she didn't force herself to concentrate on something else. And that something else was getting Matty to bed and asleep. She caught movement from the corner of her eye. It was the same dumpy, middle-aged woman she remembered checking her in the first time had entered the office. Sarah could see her moving around the shabby space turning off the TV above the counter, then the computer monitor. She came out from behind the desk, heading for the sign in the window. If she didn't get out of the van now the woman would lock the door and go to bed, leaving her and Matty stranded out in the cold.

"I don't like it here. I want to go home. I want Nate. I want my dad."

Sarah stared at her son's tear-streaked, unhappy face. What had she done, taking him away from what was familiar and comforting on Christmas Eve of all nights? "So do I," she whispered.

She didn't need time alone to contemplate her future. It was staring her in the face. She and Matty alone in the world. That's not the future she wanted for her son. It wasn't what she wanted for herself, not when there was a chance, even a very small one, to reclaim her husband. The vacancy sign flickered and went out.

She'd waited too long. Or perhaps just long enough. "We're going home, Matty." She had been wrong to run away. She had known that the moment she walked out the door of Nate's trailer, but shock at his revelation, and then hurt pride, had kept her putting one foot in front of the other, kept her walking away from Nate instead of turning to run back into his arms.

Sarah fumbled in her purse for her Christmas cell phone and flipped it open. Nothing. No lights. No beeps or chirps. The battery needed to be charged. She stared down at the piece of useless high-tech gadgetry, then shut the cover.

"Okay, I get the hint," she said aloud as she dropped the phone back in her purse. "You can't save a marriage over the phone. At least Nate and I can't. You have to do it toe-to-toe, face-to-face." And she did want to save her marriage. No matter how painful it was knowing she would never carry Nate's child, it was nothing compared to the agony of spending the rest of her life without him.

The sleet had turned to snow while they sat in the motel parking lot, adding a new layer of slickness to the roads, making driving even more treacherous. She was impatient to get back to Riley's Cove, but her eagerness had to take second place to Matty's safety. There was no traffic after she turned off the highway. She and Matty might have been the last two people on earth. She drove slowly but with growing confidence. She was more than halfway to the Cottonwood Lake turnoff when she saw the pickup in the ditch ahead of her, its headlights shining up into the trees at the side of the road.

Sarah slowed as she approached the disabled vehicle, dread tightening her stomach into a queasy knot. The pickup was the same make and model as Nate's, she realized. Her heart began to hammer in her chest. There was a man in the truck but she couldn't tell if he was conscious or unconscious, dead or alive. She pulled to a stop and rolled down her window for a better look. She wanted to leap out of the van and rush to see if Nate's lifeless body was slumped over the wheel, but she was a woman alone with a defenseless child in the middle of the night, in the middle of nowhere. She couldn't afford to be so impulsive. As she hesitated, the truck's headlights were doused and the driver's side door opened. A familiar figure emerged from the cab.

"Nate." Sarah unclasped her seat belt and jumped out of the van, almost sliding underneath it when her feet hit the slippery asphalt.

"Sarah? Is that you? Stay where you are," he said. "There's water in the bottom of the ditch."

She hung onto the door handle to keep from sliding down the embankment. "Are you all right? Are you hurt?"

"I'm fine."

"What happened? Did you hit a deer or a patch of ice?"

"A little of both." He jumped over the marshy bottom of the shallow drainage ditch, landing with a grunt, and climbed up the other side, grabbing handfuls of dried grass to pull himself up the icy incline.

And then he was beside her breathing hard but seemingly otherwise unharmed, strong and solid and safe, and she wanted more than anything for him to take her in his arms, but he didn't.

"What were you doing out here, Nate?" she whispered, both hope and dread at his answer warring inside her.

"I was coming to look for you."

"How did you know where to find us?"

"I didn't. I took a chance you'd go back to the motel."

"We did."

"Why didn't you stay?" She could feel his gaze on her face but it was too dark for her to gauge his expression.

"Matty wanted to come home," she said simply, although it took all the courage she could muster. "And so did I."

Nate did take her in his arms then, gathered her close to his heart, and she knew, with a blinding flash of certainty, it would all come out right for them somehow. "Let's go home," he said. "We have a lot to talk about."

CHAPTER NINETEEN

SARAH LEFT the bedroom, where she'd stayed with Matty until he fell asleep, and walked through the kitchen, her arms crossed beneath her breasts to hold in her nervousness. Nate was standing beside their small tree, staring out into the pre-dawn darkness of Christmas morning. The black slacks and cream-colored chamois shirt he'd worn that evening out-lined his broad shoulders and narrow waist in the pale glitter of the tree lights.

"Is Matty asleep?" he asked as she moved to stand beside him. He didn't turn to take her in his arms but gazed at the little tree. To spare Matty any more anxiety they hadn't spoken during the drive back to the trailer. She had come home, but the barriers between them had yet to be torn down and destroyed.

"He's sound asleep. At first he didn't want to close his eyes because he was afraid he'd wake up back in the van."

He laid whatever he was holding on a tree branch,

shoved his hands in his pockets, and turned toward her. "The poor little guy's had quite a night."

"He was so angry with me when he saw where we were going. I didn't realize how much he had disliked living in that motel room until I took him back there tonight."

"He'll forget all about it when he wakes up and finds Santa's been here."

"I hope so. Pleading temporary insanity doesn't carry much weight with a three-year-old who wants to be home waiting for Santa." She couldn't keep the remorse out of her voice and didn't try. "He wanted to come home so badly, Nate." she whispered, because her throat was tight with unshed tears.

"Is that why you turned around and came back?"

Sarah caught her breath. What she said next might possibly be the most important words she ever spoke. "I came back because I love you. Why did you come after us?"

"I came after you because I wanted you safe."

"You're saying knight-in-shining-armor syndrome is all it was? Another rescue mission for a woman and child in distress?"

Nate reached out and put his hands on her shoulders, but he didn't draw her into his arms. "I'm no knight. If I was I'd have let you go this time, too, set you free to find a man to love who would give you children. I'm just trying not to make the same mis-

takes I did in the past, but that doesn't mean the outcome's going to be any different, Sarah. It doesn't
mean we can save this marriage any more than we
could save our first one."

"We never had a chance to really learn about each
other before." She put her hand on his chest, over his
heart and took strength from the steady beat beneath
her fingers. "We were both to blame. Your problem
was trying to shoulder all the responsibility, make
decisions for both of us. Mine was being so uncertain of who I was that I couldn't stand up to you and
tell you that always being the one in charge was right
for the military but wrong for our relationship."

"But that doesn't explain what's happening now.
I didn't tell you that I could never make you pregnant because I knew I'd make a mess of it, possibly
force you into doing exactly what you did."

"Run away, you mean? I was wrong to do that.
I've tried so hard to become the best person I can be,
Nate. But there will always be part of me that's still
lost and lonely. Sometimes she takes over. But not
very often, and not for very long."

"And you can stand here and look me in the eye
and tell me it doesn't matter that we won't have any
more children? No brothers or sisters for Matty?"

"It matters very much," she said softly. "It breaks
my heart that we can never feel the joy of bringing
a child we made together into the world. But it

doesn't make a difference in how I feel about you. I love you, Nate. I will always love you." She reached up and pressed her lips to his.

He resisted for a moment, then with a groan he began to kiss her back. The kiss was hard and deep and drugging. When his mouth left hers they were both gasping for breath. His voice was a low, heady growl, his breath warm against her ear. "I need you, Sarah. Here. Now."

She needed him, too. She pulled her sweater over her head, let it drop to the floor, worked at the buttons of his shirt as his hands went to his belt. He unclasped her bra and she felt the cool night air on her breasts followed by his mouth on her skin. She sighed in pleasure as he lowered her to the couch, dealt with the rest of their clothes. She welcomed his heat and his weight as he settled on top of her. "I love you," she whispered as they came together. "I love you just the way you are."

"SARAH, WAKE UP. We should go to bed. Or at least get our clothes on. It will be dawn soon and Matty won't sleep long after that."

"Can't we stay here just a little longer?" she asked, reaching up to find his mouth with her lips.

"Maybe just a little longer," he murmured.

When he woke the second time it was full daylight. "Sarah, wake up. We really have overslept this time." He raised up on one elbow and kissed her on both eyelids.

She opened her eyes and smiled up at him, a sleepy, contented smile, that he no longer had to imagine he was seeing. "What time is it?" His right hand was lying on her breast. She turned his wrist and looked at his watch.

"*Seven-thirty.* Matty will be up soon. We should put some clothes on." He'd pulled one of his mother's crocheted afghans over them during the night, but it had fallen to the floor the last time they made love. He scooped it up and covered her with it, reaching down to drag on his clothes, not wanting to spend Christmas morning explaining to Matty why he and Sarah were sleeping naked on the couch. Sarah tucked the throw around her, depriving him of the sight of her breasts. She looked sated and relaxed and beautiful.

"We need to finish what we started last night." He sat down on the edge of the couch.

"I don't need more explanations, Nate. I understand how hard it was for you to tell me something so personal—"

"It was personal until we made our sham marriage real. From that moment on it was important to us as a couple." He laced his hands between his knees, stared down at his bare feet. She waited silently, giving him the time he needed to find the right words.

"I didn't mean to keep my condition a secret, I swear. Circumstances just conspired against me. I called my doctor for an appointment right away so that I could have all the facts ready to explain to you. That's where I hit the first snag. He's on temporary active duty in Iraq. He won't be back in the States until March." She scooted up against the cushions.

"And you thought it would be at least that long before I got nervous about not being pregnant?"

"Yes," he said. He smiled ruefully. "I should have known better. Patience was never part of your personality."

"I've learned patience about some things because I've had no choice," she said, reaching out to run her fingers through his hair. "But I'm still very impulsive about the things I want very, very badly."

"Like becoming pregnant?"

"Not just becoming pregnant, but pregnant with our child," she corrected him.

She turned her head to kiss the palm of his hand. "I told you last night having a child together or not doesn't make any difference to how I feel about you, even though I do mourn the unfairness of it. I love you, Nate. Today. Tomorrow. Always."

"And I love you." He bent to kiss her mouth. It was getting easier now, letting her into the private places of his heart. "There's something else I've been thinking about, something I want to tell you."

"What's that?" She held his face between her hands so that their lips remained within inches of each other.

"Mommy? Nate?" He'd been too immersed in the new foundation of trust that was taking shape between them to pay attention to the telltale waking sounds from Matty's bedroom.

"Oh, dear, I don't want him to see me like this," Sarah said, her eyes growing large.

Nate helped her to her feet, angling himself between her and Matty's line of sight, as she wiggled into her skirt and sweater. He buttoned his shirt as she shoved her bra and pantyhose under the couch with her foot. "Don't let me forget they're there," she whispered with a mischievous grin, running her fingers through her hair. He realized he'd never seen her look quite so carefree and happy.

"How do I look?"

"Like you made love to your husband on the couch all night."

"That bad, huh?"

"Matty won't notice. Not when he sees all his presents."

"His presents. Santa." She whirled around to stare at the tree. "And my camera. Where is it?"

"It's on the counter where you left it. Here he comes." Nate grinned. "Go on, sidetrack him for a minute while I deal with the milk and cookies Santa forgot to eat."

It was over an hour before all the gifts were opened and Matty had settled down in front of the tree to play with his toys while Sarah started breakfast.

"What can I do to help?" Nate asked, as he finished tidying up and shoved the last of the crumpled wrapping paper into the wastebasket beside the sink.

"You can make the cocoa," she said. "It's your specialty. I wouldn't dream of invading your turf." She was wearing a pair of gray flannel drawstring pants and a matching Henley, and he suspected she wasn't wearing any underwear beneath the soft, clinging fabric. He watched her crack eggs into a bowl and the gentle sway of her hips and breasts made him wonder how long it would be before they could coax Matty into a nap?

"Sarah, look." Nate pointed toward the living area with the spoon he was using to make hot chocolate. Matty was wearing his child-size tool belt, hammer and screwdrivers and wrenches protruding from each loop, busily sizing up the coffee table with his little tape measure. "What do you suppose he's got in mind?"

"I'm hoping he's going to try to saw it in two," Sarah giggled. "It's way too big."

"Hey, it came with the couch and chair. It's a matched set."

Sarah gave an inelegant little snort. "So I noticed."

"I suppose you'll be wanting brand-new furniture when we move into the barn."

"Of course," she said, whisking eggs, her new sapphire catching flashes of light from the bright winter sun shining through the window above the sink. "Pine, I think. With a lot of chintz. Very country chic."

"Country chic?" He didn't like the sound of that. "We'll see. But we can't get rid of everything. We'll have a lot of space to fill. Especially with five bedrooms."

Her hand stilled above the mixing bowl. "Five bedrooms? The original plans only show three." Her brow furrowed as she concentrated on recalling the details of the renovation sketches.

She put down the whisk and turned to face him, the little frown still wrinkling her forehead, her brown eyes puzzled. The kitchen was so small he could reach out and pull her into his arms without taking a step but he didn't, not just yet. "Why on earth would we need five bedrooms for just the three of us?"

"Not just the three of us, Sarah. That's what else I wanted to tell you this morning." He couldn't keep his hands off her a moment more. He reached out and smoothed away the furrow between her eyes with the pad of his thumb. "But then Matty woke up and there hasn't been time since."

"What did you want to tell me?"

He took a deep breath. He wanted to get this right. "I've been thinking. Maybe we can't have a baby of our own, but there are dozens, hundreds of kids out there, caught in the system the way you were, kids who need a home and a family. I thought maybe we could find a place for two or three of them here with us."

"Oh, Nate. Do you mean it? Becase I was going to suggest the same thing. It came to me in the night. Offer our home, a real home, and our love to kids who don't have either." She closed her eyes and he could see she was trying not to cry. That was something else he intended to treat differently in this marriage. He would always hate to see her cry, but now he knew that tears weren't always a bad thing.

"Don't fight it, Sarah," he said, cupping her face in his hands. "You can cry as much as you want to. As long as they're happy tears."

She opened her eyes and crystal drops chased themselves down her cheeks. "They are." She kissed him quick and hard, wrapping her arms around his waist and squeezing so hard he grunted in surprise.

"So you think the idea has merit?" he asked dryly, looking over the top of her head at Matty, who was paying them no attention whatsoever. He was too engrossed in attempting to cut the bottom leg off the coffee table with his toothless saw.

She lifted her radiant face to his. "It's brilliant. We should take as many as we can. I've told you and told that you'll make a great father. Now, instead of two or three children, we can have dozens and dozens."

He laughed. "You think we'd be good at this foster parent thing, huh?" He tried to keep his voice light, but deep inside he wanted and needed her affirmation.

"We'll be great at it," she said with complete and utter confidence, and turned back to her eggs.

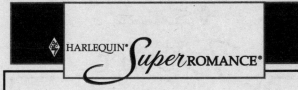

HARLEQUIN *Super*ROMANCE®

Critically acclaimed author

Tara Taylor Quinn

brings you

The Promise of Christmas

Harlequin Superromance #1309
On sale November 2005

In this deeply emotional story, a woman
unexpectedly becomes the guardian of her
brother's child. Shortly before Christmas,
Leslie Sanderson finds herself coping with
grief, with lingering and fearful memories and
with unforseen motherhood. She also
rediscovers a man from her past who could
help her move toward the promise
of a new future....

Available wherever Harlequin books are sold.

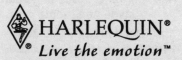

HARLEQUIN®
® *Live the emotion*™

HARLEQUIN *Super*ROMANCE®

HOMETOWN
◆ U.S.A. ◆

An Unlikely Match
by Cynthia Thomason

Harlequin Superromance #1312
On sale November 2005

She's the mayor of Heron Point. He's an
uptight security expert. When Jack Hogan
tells Claire Betancourt that her little town
of artisans and free spirits has a security
problem, sparks fly! Then her daughter goes
missing, and Claire knows that Jack is the
man to bring her safely home.

*Available wherever
Harlequin books are sold.*

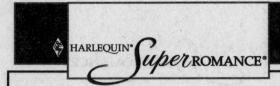
HARLEQUIN *Super*ROMANCE®

A powerful new story from a
RITA® Award-nominated author!

A Year and a Day
by Inglath Cooper

Harlequin Superromance #1310
On sale November 2005

Audrey Colby's life is the envy of most. She's
married to a handsome, successful man, she
has a sweet little boy and they live in a lovely
home in an affluent neighborhood. But
everything is not always as it seems. Only
Nicholas Wakefiled has seen the danger
Audrey's in. Instead of helping, though,
he complicates things even more....

Available wherever Harlequin books are sold.

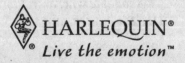
HARLEQUIN®
Live the emotion™